THE
FOREST AND
THE **CROWS**

THE FOREST AND THE CROWS

FIRST BOOK IN
A SONG OF NIALLA

A TALE   BEYOND RETURN

MATIAN ELLIS
OSCUR BELLOC

ISBN: 979-8-9892029-4-2 (Ebook)
ISBN: 979-8-9892029-2-8 (Paperback)
ISBN: 979-8-9892029-3-5 (Hardcover)

Any references to historical events, real people, or places are used fictitiously. Names, characters, and places are products of the author's imagination.

Cover, illustration, and layout design by Brandon Richard Collebrusco

Second Edition, 2024.

www.matianellis.com

For those young artists,
who learn from their mistakes,
and never give up on their dreams.

CONTENTS

AUTHOR'S NOTE

The Forest and the Crows was originally published in January 2020 as a novella detailing the beginning of Nialla Elendsah's narrative for *A Tale Beyond Return*, the series. This rendition is the Second Edition, with large portions of the text re-written and the lore expanded to include alterations to the world setting as it will appear in the third installment, *The Wolves on a Yellow Field*. Changes include names of characters and locations the author felt were important for the reader, along with new illustrations and artwork to represent a better version of the author's dark fantasy universe.

A Tale Beyond Return is an expansive world inspired by real-world mythologies. The contents of this book are the product of the author's imagination, and the resemblance to the names of people, locations, or events in the real world is unintended and coincidental.

An important note concerning the primary female character, Nialla Elendsah: due to her nature—born of ellúndar, vedreron, aenúmorian, and human lines—she appears much younger than her personality's maturity would figure. At the onset of this story, Nialla is roughly sixty-five years old but has the younger appearance of six. The cause of this discrepancy is that her mother's people, the Ellúndar (best equivalent to Mountain Elves), are an extortionary long-live race with a slower age progression. As it is the author's preference, Nialla ages physically at the rate of one year for every ten years. However, after such a life, her mind has already experienced more than most human adults but retains a childlike demeanor.

Other characters, such as Sackery of the Vedrethal, a natural-born Aenúmorian with a lifespan of only a couple centuries, are alive far beyond the capacity of his people due to events of his past, which unnaturally prolonged his life beyond the normal for his kind.

M.E.O.B.

MAPS

OF

THE

VALLEY

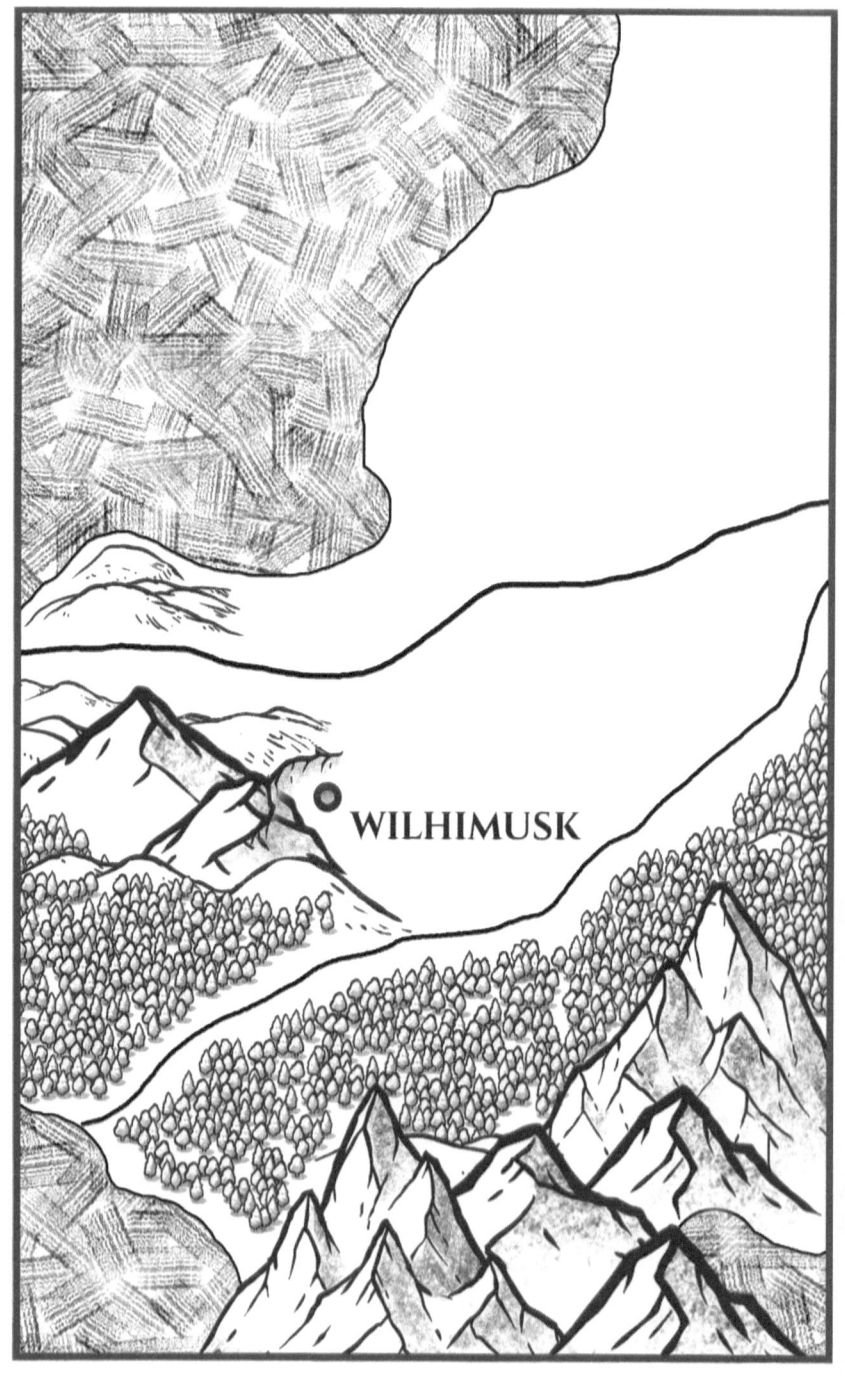

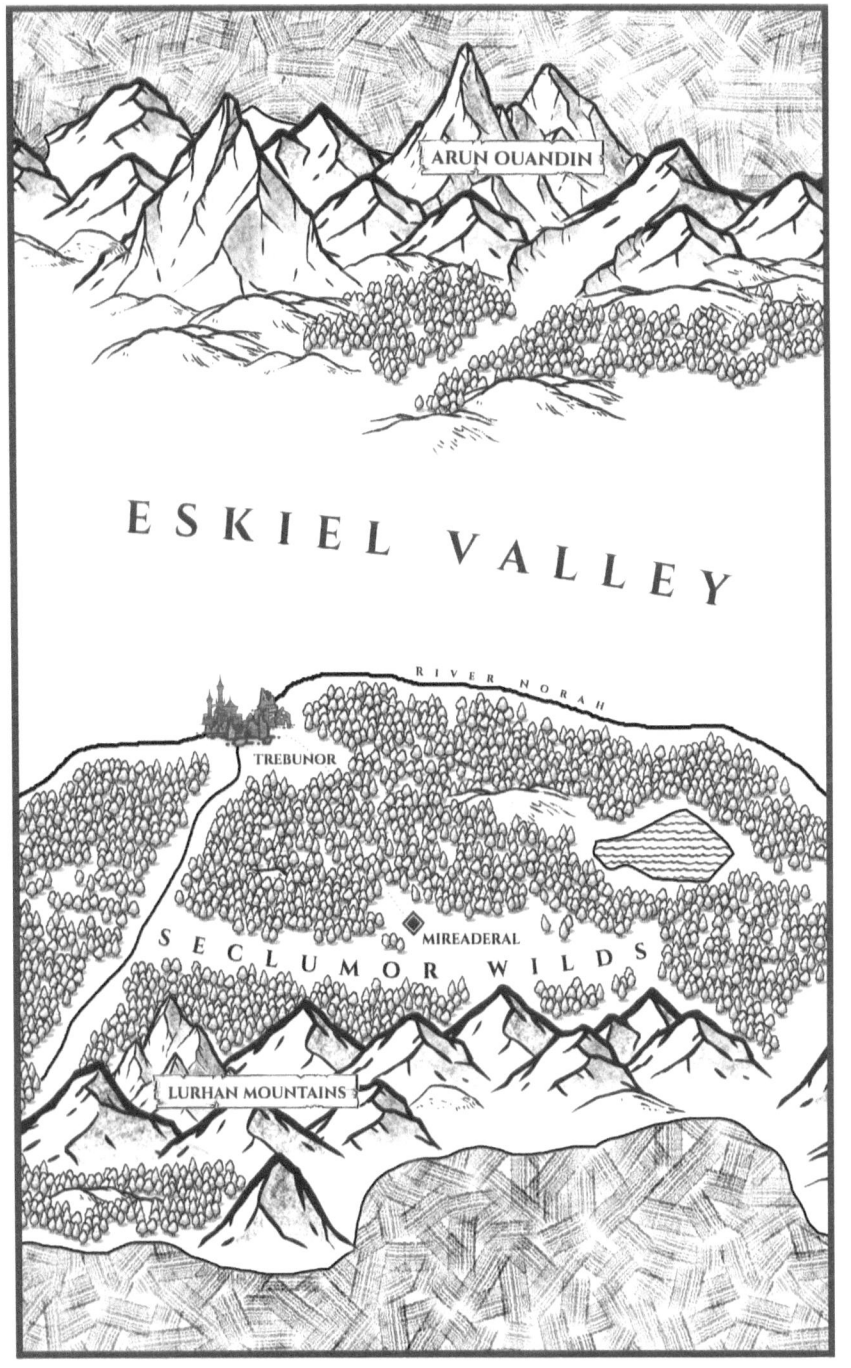

THE FOREST AND THE CROWS

A TALE BEYOND RETURN

BY

MATIAN ELLIS

— Arún Ouandin, Eskiel Valley —

1169 SE

65 Years After the War of His Return.

Endúcar, King of Calidor, had died in his defeat of the
dragon Morenarch at the Battle of Aardan.
His beloved, Cyridel Elendsah, Princess of Ilhivendal,
had a child on the battle's eve—a little girl, Nialla.
Before his death, Endúcar asked one of his
warrior-servants and oathsworn friend,
Sackery of the Vedrethal,
to protect them from his would-be enemies.

— 1 —

THE LONG ROAD

Fate often brings tragic circumstances that can lead the fearful and lost down uncertain paths to their destinations.

Sackery presses his palm to the ground. Even with the wind stealing his breath as they climb higher into the mountains, he can spot the trail well enough under the snow. It's an old and narrow path, once trodden on by thousands, but now a forgotten route through Arún Ouandin.

He wonders how much history is under all this ice.

Cyridel climbs up next to him, a steady rhythm to her chest. She raises her arm to protect her eyes as the air turns hard against them.

"Where is she?!" she asks, pulling her cloak down to her nose.

"She's run ahead," he tells her.

"And you didn't stop her?"

Sackery frowns. "If a blizzard doesn't slow the girl, what makes you think I can?" he asks, huffing into his palms to win back some warmth. He looks forward and sees a small figure standing amid the flurries. Nialla has a stiff, upright stance, her arms outstretched, letting the wind flow around her, untouched.

"What is she doing?!" Cyridel shouts.

"Letting the storm take her!" Sackery laughs. "Don't worry! She can hardly feel it!"

The wind knocks him back a few steps. Sackery leverages his weight and manages to dig his heels into the ground. Cyridel grabs his arm, grounding him as the air fights their steps up the mountain. It isn't easy to imagine anybody coming this way, even to flee north, as the Maithandír once had—Cyridel's kindred, who became the Míran.

But the three of them are heading south, away from the petty kingdoms that've cropped up across the continent in the years since they left. Nialla was a baby then, and Cyridel wanted to honor the girl's father by taking her away from a world still reeling from a war that saw a king lost, a myth reborn, a dragon killed . . . And a hope that comes from the unexpected.

After sixty-five years, they've all grown a little older.

Cyridel huddles next to Sackery as they reach a rocky alcove that gives them a moment's reprieve. All the while, Nialla stands at the crest above them, unaware of how much they struggle to keep pace with her as she darts into the heaviest of the snow.

"She doesn't even feel the damn cold," Sackery curses under his breath.

She has her father's hot blood and her mother's light foot.

Cyridel's normally pale skin flushes red as she sticks her nose out from under her hood. She looks at him with a faint sadness. Sackery has traveled with the woman long enough to recognize her glances, even when she pretends to bury her emotions deeper every year.

"We can't stay out here," Cyridel tells him.

"I know," Sackery agrees.

"My father's stories said they took shelter in caves they found along the way."

"And you want *us* to look for one?"

"Do we have another choice?"

Sackery turns so the wind hits his back instead of his face. "No."

The two drag themselves out of cover to a sharply curved terrace with a steep drop rolling down one side, where Nialla waits.

"Nialla!" Cyridel calls to her.

Sackery cuffs his hands around his mouth. "Nells! Can you hear us?"

Nialla nods her response.

They've spent the girl's life in the wilderness and on the run, surviving off the land, often sheltered by decent people as they go from village to town. Sackery finds that wholesome. No matter how poor or ill-weathered, folks like to come together and offer hospitality to strangers. He doesn't know if it's because the people in his day were less trustful of others or if it's simply them pitying two drifters with a young child nuzzled against her mother's chest.

"Something's over there!" Nialla calls back, a finger pointing in the distance.

"Something?" Sackery returns.

"A light? A cold light," Nialla murmurs. "Colder than the snow."

Sackery can barely hear her over the gales curling his ears. He grabs ahold of the rockface and climbs to her, but the farther he goes, the harder it is to breathe. Nialla meets him at the ledge when he makes it to the top, a hair more than a giant is tall above the old trail.

"Can you still see it?" Sackery begs the question, folding his arms under his cloak.

Nialla nods.

Sackery gives her a nudge and takes her hand before finding a way down to Cyridel. Pushing ahead, he walks with a hand on his sword belt. A light in these parts should be impossible . . . Nobody's lived in these lands since these mountains marked the border of the old Maithandír kingdom of Invala Dailn. Sackery's eyes narrow as he attempts to see past the flurries, though the snow's too thick to make out anything more than an arm's length away.

Nialla marches ahead again without saying another word.

She moves too quickly through the snow for Sackery to stop her. "Nialla!" he yells, but the violent gust mutes the sound of his voice. It's like what she did at Eradbin, only now they are battling a storm, not the empty fortress halls of Duakon Kûral.

Sackery rushes after her, gasping for what little air he can get.

In a loud crack, the storm quiets to a slow, lumbering snowfall. A fragile calmness replaces the violent winds. Sackery catches a glimpse of the girl awash against a brilliant white sky.

Nialla smiles and winks at him, jumping off the trail and running farther ahead.

"Don't fall behind!" she hollers.

Sackery looks at Cyridel with an unnerving ire—a look she mirrors, and for good reason.

Nialla should know better than to pluck the strings to disrupt the weather. But what can they do? Sackery watched as her forebearers tore down mountains and changed the course of rivers to win battles . . . All because they *could*, rattling the natural balance of the music that shapes all life in a reactive world.

Nothing was ever enough. And that makes Sackery afraid, knowing how easily she can fall into the same traps.

They find Nialla again at a bend in the rocks where the snow goes shallow, and the path widens.

Sackery hurries and tugs at her shoulder, only to realize what she meant by a cold light. "Headstones?"

She's led them into an old burial ground. The graves are hard to see, buried by the frequent snowfall in these mountains. Some have their tops uncovered, most likely by the recent winds. And of those Sackery can see, they all have a common shape, like small mounds.

"So many of them," Nialla points out.

"Dozens," Cyridel counts, walking the length.

"A long way to come to bury the dead," Sackery notions. "And here? Why?"

"I don't know," Cyridel admits.

Nialla doesn't speak. Sackery can tell by the hard stare on the girl's face that she's now feeling a chill.

"Are you alright?" he asks her.

The girl upturns her gaze to him and frowns.

"It's quiet . . . I don't remember it being so quiet before," Nialla mourns.

"The dead don't speak, Nells," Sackery tells her.

Nialla shakes her head. "Not the graves. It's like I hear, I hear—?" She takes in a breath and lets it out. "Everything's softer here."

"Softer?"

"Suffocating?"

"We *are* very high," Sackery tells her.

"No. It's like I am drowning," the girl shudders.

Cyridel calls to them. "Over here! Take a look at this!"

Sackery squeezes Nialla's arm, pulling the girl away to rejoin her mother.

"What is it?" he asks Cyridel.

"Another grave," Cyridel answers. "Less worn than the others."

Sackery kneels next to her and rests his hand on the crux of the sphere. "Something's carved at the top," he reads, brushing off the snow, finding flatter stones around the base. Etched symbols mark the perimeter, the words branching out in an elegant pattern, or would've had time not eaten away at the edges.

"Names and dates," Cyridel describes,

"It's written in Aarendelic," Sackery understands.

"A slightly different vernacular than what I am used to," Cyridel admits. "Older? Done with care."

"Can you read it?" Sackery asks.

"Mostly. Less than I should," Cyridel confesses. "Some of these words?"

"These are the graves of your kin," Sackery realizes.

Cyridel nods. "Death poems to entertain their watchful rest," she offers.

"They must've died on their journey north," Sackery alludes. "And they're all like this?" He wanders to another gravestone, clearing off more of the snow.

Cyridel walks over as he traces the letters with his fingertips.

"Is this what my father meant? He was a boy when my grandfather led the long march through these mountains," Cyridel illustrates. "I've heard so many stories . . . But this? These people must've died lost and hungry, wanting to find a new home. I never believed how bad it was. Always just stories, I thought."

Nialla approaches her mother, calm and collected—a demeanor beyond her apparent years.

"Their memory survives," Sackery whispers.

Much of the past rarely matches the stories parents tell their children.

Cyridel offers a prayer to the graves left behind by her grandfather. She speaks of better days and the lives these people never saw in Ilhivendal—white peaks stretching over a vibrant river vale, little streams flowing alongside the streets and under bridges connecting the grand towers of her city's vast reaches.

Nialla tugs on her mother's sleeve.

Cyridel takes her daughter's hand and stands. "It won't be long before we're in the valley."

"Do your stories tell you that?" Sackery asks.

"No. You can see where the mountains drop from this perch."

Sackery frowns. He's learned to trust her senses. It's not a power. Her eyes are sharper than his. And on clear weather days, she can see details that escape him.

Nialla walks to the edge and stares over the slopes.

Sackery wraps an arm around her. "What are you looking at?"

"I don't know. I thought I heard something?" Nialla describes. "A voice on the air?" She swallows. "Or maybe the wind." The girl breaks away and steps onto a rise for a better view. "But I *do* see a tower! Maybe another light? Warmer this time."

Sackery doesn't see it, but the girl *did* inherit her mother's keen sense. He parcels a few odd shapes and a glow in the distance. His best guess is that the light is merely a caustic mirage of the sun reflecting off the ice on the mountaintops.

He lifts Nialla onto his shoulders. "You'll have to teach me how you two see so far someday."

"Maybe we will?" Cyridel laughs, throwing back her hood to reveal her ears. "Or maybe not. You're still a good tracker."

"Years of practice to train the muscles," Sackery murmurs. "But I am only here to kill things for you."

"You are more than *that* to us," the woman hints, but she looks away, suddenly quiet.

Sackery is very good at killing men and monsters alike. Yet it's not like Cyridel hasn't done her share over the years. He glances at the long daggers sticking out the top fold of her pack. Sackery recalls her stabbing a soldier who threatened to take her daughter away when they were traveling through Esgrelion a few years ago, passing by the city of Orwynswall.

Nialla looked much the same then as she does now, not that it surprises him anymore.

He's long dealt with people who are stronger and smarter than him.

The life of a Vedrethal is one dedicated to a duty that endures for as long as he can fight. Legends speak of a warrior of a bygone era, an unmatched swordsman, able to cut swathes through man and beast alike.

Sackery recoils, attributing those stories to his luck rather than his skills.

He is *unmatched* because he's still walking around, not feeding the dirt like his enemies.

On the horizon, the sun drops behind the mountains. "Night's about to whisper us a tune," Sackery expresses.

Cyridel looks up and out. "We shouldn't hold back the storm for much longer."

"And why not?" Nialla demands with the stubbornness of a cat.

Cyridel smiles at her before stepping back and toward the graves. "Because we don't know what else is out there." She walks the edge along the rocks, running a hand across, occasionally tapping the surface. Sackery watches, sinking into the snow with Nialla on his shoulders.

"And do your stories tell you where these caves are?" Sackery asks.

"They were vague on that," Cyridel iterates, digging at the rock until cracks form in the ice.

Sackery lets Nialla off his shoulders and helps Cyridel move the debris. "This isn't a cave. It's a fissure," he tells her. "Can you see how deep it goes?"

"I can't tell," Cyridel admits. "It's too dark. But I think it can last us the night."

"Odd there isn't a marker," Sackery weighs, picking up a

stone and handing it to Nialla to stack. "I'd have thought your grandfather would've taken every opportunity to guide your people to shelter."

"Were you expecting some grand sculpture?" Cyridel asks.

Sackery draws back and breathes into his hands. "No? But they had time to lay these stones."

"I wasn't here," Cyridel tells him.

"These were your people."

"And my father wasn't much older than Nialla. Stories change with retellings. Sometimes? It's to hide the mistakes taken along the way."

"Or maybe those tales should stay the same? Allow people to hear them true."

Cyridel shakes her head. "Not everybody wants to remember when they stumble."

"But our scars make us who we are, do they not?" Sackery laughs, offering his thoughts.

"Speaks the soldier who runs into every fight," Cyridel taunts him.

Sackery clears his throat. "Not every fight," he murmurs.

As they drag out the last few rocks, they lose the daylight, the sky going from white to orange. Shadows dance between the mountains. They finish making an opening large enough for all three to fit. It's a tight squeeze, but Sackery manages after snagging a strap, the rocks scraping the metal under his cloak.

As he pushes inside, the space before him gives out. He

ducks forward, breaking through a wall and hitting flatter ground.

Sackery raises his head to find pillars stretching up to a vaulted ceiling.

"I suppose that answers my question," he mutters, pushing off the floor and brushing the dust off him.

"What was that—" Cyridel says, following him into the chamber, "—noise?"

Sackery hums a soft tune before walking to one of the pillars. "They built it inside the mountain," he suggests, going to bring Nialla inside. "Now I understand why they say the world is slow to change." Nialla's face glows as she enters the chamber, a silver glint reflecting the ornate stonework. "It makes me wonder if escaping their troubles didn't cause them to feel homesick."

"I did when I first left Ilhivendal," Cyridel tells him.

"I remember what you told me. You were lost in the woods, found by a giant?"

"That was when I was a girl and stepped off the road. No. I was talking about leaving my home with a baby in my arms," Cyridel laments. "Had I known I wouldn't see it again for over sixty years?" She rubs her palms together, shivering as the cold sneaks through the entry fissure. Sackery looks away and breathes, letting her steal a moment's peace. "I don't know what I would have done."

"We don't have to go south. Should you want, we can return to Ilhivendal."

Cyridel smiles, a contour to her ivory palette.

"And risk bringing her somewhere *they* could find her? That isn't what Nialla's father wanted."

"Galron is dead, my lady," Sackery tells her. "The entire world cried for him."

"Don't you think I know that?" Cyridel shudders.

Nialla steps between them, a girl half their size but taller than a child her age should be. "This doesn't help us."

Sackery looks at the girl and chuckles. "She's right. We could settle," he offers. "Find a tack of land, build a farm? A hard life, but a quiet one."

"And where can we go that others won't follow?" Cyridel demands.

Sackery rubs the back of his neck. "Anywhere that's better than our lives these past few years," he calls her out and, after, holds his breath.

Cyridel takes a small step back and lowers her shoulders. She looks at Nialla, then back at him.

Nialla has tears frozen on her face. "Sackery? Please don't."

He draws back and feels his throat. "I am sorry," Sackery returns. "I am tired."

"Maybe it's time," Cyridel concedes.

Sackery leans against the cavern's wall and slides to the ground, worn raw to the bone.

"At least this tomb is a good shelter for us," he says.

"Let's make camp for the night and look for a way down the mountains tomorrow," Cyridel decides.

"That's the plan," Sackery agrees.

He closes his eyes and buries his face into his knees. Nialla might've stemmed the storm for a time, but once she finds a place here, it'll return worse than before. Forcing an unnatural change in nature has consequences. Sackery's counted it more than enough times to understand.

Such power tends to twist the songs into abhorrent renditions of themselves, like shadows within shadows.

Sackery opens his eyes to find Nialla sitting at his feet, staring like a fox at a bird.

"Are you sleeping?" she asks.

"Enough to catch my breath and prepare for the night's watch."

"Don't you need to run to catch something?"

Sackery sits up and sighs. "Are you calling me slow?" he asks.

"I am calling you old," she laughs.

"No older than you will be someday," he tells her.

"As long as we live longer than everybody else, does it matter?"

"Maybe not," Sackery glooms.

He looks to the crack in the wall where they entered, the daylight gone. And with it, the winds return, whistling like a flute on market day in Aldergard. Now they're stuck here until it clears.

"Are you okay?" Nialla asks him.

Even in the dark, Sackery notices the blood dripping from

the girl's nose. He takes the end of his cloak and dabs her face. Nialla resists him at first, as she usually does. "I am okay. How did this happen?" he asks.

"I hit my head on the way down," she tells him.

Sackery looks at her and cocks an eyebrow. He still forgets how much she's gone through.

"You should be more careful."

"Like you?"

"Not like me."

"Are you cold?"

"A fire should do us fine, don't you think?"

"Do we have anything to burn?"

"Some old clothes from our packs. A few odds and ends."

Cyridel joins them, speaking softly. "I can go look for firewood."

"Nothing grows up here," Sackery tells her.

"Clothes, it is, then," Nialla whimpers.

– The Crossing of Arún Ouandin –

— 2 —

IN A DARK TOMB

Cyridel nestles close to her daughter as the girl sleeps beside the low fire. It's a cavernous tomb they've found themselves in for the night. She hums to scare away whatever ghosts still linger here. Memories haunt this place—a history that can play tricks on the mind.

Howling whispers echo from the cracks in the walls.

Growing up in Ilhivendal, every child learns that ghosts are merely ideas the living attribute to a place. After a person dies, their spirit shepherds away across an eternal sea to Iánturial, where that life brings a darker aspect into paradise.

Nialla tucks her hands under her arms.

Cyridel pulls one of their blankets over the girl, letting her get cozy after days of fighting off the blizzard.

Sackery watches by the entrance with his cloak wrapped tightly around him. He paces back and forth, staying in the cold for another hour before walking in for warmth by the embers. His face looks pale and, to Cyridel's intuition, numb to the touch.

"Storm is on the rise again," he says, sitting down, huffing into his palms. "She's asleep? Probably for the best."

"She's exhausted," Cyridel tells him.

"You saw what she did," Sackery frowns.

"At least we found this place for tonight," she accepts.

"Fortunate for us that Nialla could see a cold light from the graves."

"Cold light . . . What does that even mean?"

"I don't know," Sackery admits. "I am learning there's a lot I don't know."

Cyridel remembers when they crossed the deserts in Assur—they were holed up in a ravine for days as a sandstorm battered the horizon, threatening to suffocate them. Nialla could barely walk then and relied utterly on Sackery and Cyridel to carry her from danger.

Now, they're stuck in the mountains, battling the ice and snow instead of the vast dunes and the sand dragons that burrow underneath them.

Sackery looks heavily at her with deep, blue eyes.

"You should get some rest," she tells him.

"I am not tired," he chuckles.

"You look it."

"It could be my age catching up with me," he scoffs.

"And I know a girl less stubborn than you," Cyridel scolds.

Sackery looks on at the slumbering Nialla. The girl's chest beats softly under the blanket, undoubtedly listening to their conversation. The Daughter of the Mountains had inherited her parents' curiousness, often coupled with a temper as severe as a hurricane in springtime.

"Get some rest," Cyridel reiterates.

The man quietly gets up and steps to one of the intricately carved murals on the tomb's walls.

"Cyridel. What is this place?" he asks her.

She follows him and presses her palm to the stones. "A refuge?" she weighs.

"For us? Of course. But what about the people who built it?"

There is an old aarendelic inscription that dresses the edge of the images. Cyridel counts twelve figures carved into the wall, nearly equal distance apart. Etchings represent the base forms of wind, earth, and water, each flowing into a single, almost dance-like form.

Sackery moves aside to allow her a fuller view of it.

Only some writing remains intact after weathering so many storms over the years.

She traces the letterforms with her fingers, whispering their meanings.

"I don't understand," Cyridel admits.

"What is it?"

"A name? Lambárd," Cyridel reads. "It repeats? A story written in lyrics." She moves past the words and looks at the paintings by the pillars. "Falling stars streak across a blood-red sky—outlying fires. People huddle together, keeping warm. Others? Driven through by cold steel. Many ran, but from what?"

"Which way are the stars falling?" Sackery asks.

"I don't . . . It doesn't show," Cyridel shudders. "But . . . Here? Do you see?"

"A central figure?"

"Figures. Three of them," Cyridel weighs. "Crows . . . Sitting on a tree. All the others?"

"They're facing them," Sackery notices.

"Weapons drawn."

"Blood?"

"A depiction of a battle," Cyridel realizes.

"Against what? These birds?"

"Maybe? Ellúndar built these walls."

"We don't know if it was your grandfather," Sackery alludes.

"It could've been . . . Or maybe it was another group? Folks that came after, following his footsteps."

Sackery drifts forward and blocks the light. "A warning?" he suggests.

"A lot of work to tell people to stay away," Cyridel refuses.

"Not many ways through these mountains," Sackery explains.

"But why not write a clear message?" Cyridel weighs. "Why bury it under the rock?"

"Maybe it wasn't always buried?" Sackery implies.

"Maybe," Cyridel recedes.

"A lot of maybes," Sackery dithers.

"Too many," she agrees.

They return to the fire and warm their hands. All this talk of warnings and the past wears on Cyridel, much like rust eats at iron, slowly rotting it away from the outside. And that leaves a pain in her chest, knowing she's so close and yet so far from the place she was born.

All to keep a promise to a man whose face she can't even remember anymore.

But the girl has *his* eyes, like the water in the fountains of Ilhivendal.

Sackery breaks the silence. "The question is," the man says, "where do we go from here?"

Cyridel brings her knees up to her chin. "What do you mean?"

"We can't survive in the wilderness for good," Sackery instigates. "Somewhere out there is safe enough for us!"

"We've attempted that before," Cyridel reminds him. "Have we ever found safety?"

Sackery's gaze falls groundward. "No more than countless others," he notions.

"And no fewer," Cyridel agrees.

"Wherever we go, there'll always be those who'll recognize *what* she is," Sackery warns.

"And staying in one place will only attract *more* unwanted danger."

"We'd be able to stand from a stronger position," the old Vedrethal states. "On the road, we're venturing into territories we don't know. We've been lucky for years. How long do you think that luck will last?"

"It'll be dangerous," Cyridel echoes.

"Always being on the move, never staying anywhere for long . . . How is *that* not dangerous?" Sackery argues. Nialla stirs where she lies, and he smiles at the girl's attempt to pretend otherwise. "We know you're not asleep, little one. Might as well join the debate, wouldn't you say?"

Nialla sits up and stares at the pair intently. Her silver eyes are dark against the fire's faint glow.

Cyridel quickly wraps her arm around the girl and brings her in close.

Nialla pulls away and folds her arms. "And what if we *do* settle down? Tell me."

"They could find us," Cyridel answers.

"Because they don't know anything else," Sackery explains.

"And if they find us, what will happen to them?" Nialla iterates.

Sackery and Cyridel both fall quiet at the question.

Nialla outstretches a hand and looks at the fire, the embers glowing brighter the longer she stares.

"The first thing I remember is waking up to a thunderstorm as we hid inside a cave," the girl says, shadows on her face as she looks away and the fire dims. "I don't know why I remember it, but I do. And I remember I was crying. Not sad, but . . . happy? I always loved the smell of rain after that, the flowers in meadows, the way the grass comes alive after."

Cyridel sits up as Nialla's lips go thin. She doesn't say another word. Would it make a difference if she did?

"Storms always followed us after that," Sackery utters. "Now I know why."

Nialla faintly smiles. She wraps her hand around the stone she wears—a small trinket that had belonged to her father, but one that illuminates the dark when she touches it. The flames crack and pop as Cyridel lifts a blanket around their shoulders, the fire battling the wind outside for dominance.

Cyridel touches her own necklace, the Fallenstar of June—a jewel given to her the day they named her.

She recalls the white-stone bridges that stretch between the houses on the slopes that rise with the mountain heights. Today, those memories remain in her dreams. Pleasant. Cyridel would dance in the pools that dot the courtyards from the waterfalls to the little rivers crowded by ferryboats brimming with lovers on warm spring days. And of all the grand structures, she'd like to see the Summit Hall again, the highest reaches of the kingdom-city.

"We should not linger on the past," Cyridel mourns.

Nialla perks her ears as Sackery turns his head from the fireside.

Cyridel returns with a sullen frown.

"Do you mean it?" the girl asks.

"Nialla," Cyridel whispers.

"We've walked a long way to get here," Sackery notions.

"To the edges of the world and back," Cyridel agrees.

"I don't understand," Nialla murmurs.

Cyridel untucks her legs and turns to her daughter, taking the girl's hands and running her thumb over her weather-beaten knuckles.

"You know I still yearn for my home in Ilhivendal?" Cyridel asks, nabbing a waterskin from her pack to wash the girl's palms. "After all this time, I wouldn't know what I'd do if I hadn't those memories to bring me the joy of when I was young."

"What are you trying to say?" Nialla begs the question.

"Sweet girl? You never had that chance for a life as I did," Cyridel tells her.

The girl bites her lip and suddenly looks away. "Somewhere to call home?" Nialla asks.

Cyridel sees the light flickering in her daughter's eyes. A quiet moment hangs in the air until Sackery offers her a nod.

"Somewhere to call home," she agrees, kissing the girl on the forehead.

Dropping back into her covers and listening to the empty air, Cyridel wonders about the chances of seeing her *home* again. Would they recognize her? Do they even care? Her kindred have long memories. But no matter their centuries-old experiences, her people never understood how quickly the world could change. Is she the same person who used to listen to the Storyteller at night? Is she that lost child in the woods a giant found and carried back to her father?

Her name is Cyridel Elendsah—Daughter of Ilhivendal and child of Lurón and Nadrial.

Descended of two worlds, the Sydaunaen Ellúndar of Invala Dailn, known as the Maithandír, later called the Míran after the Long March of her grandfather, Galronallin. And then, there is the other quarter, the Aenümorian, the race to which Sackery once belonged many years before the Vedreron adopted *him* and others *like* him as the first of the Vedrethal.

Those days of gentler songs have now passed, along with any world that made sense.

— 3 —

AN OLD DEAD TONGUE

Nialla is the first to wake up and sneaks away, crawling through the crack that leads out of the tomb. She enjoys her hair flying as the air hits it right. Nialla closes her eyes and embraces the dying bellows of the blizzard as it passes with the young sunrise. Outside, she can be free.

Her attempts to stall yesterday's storm left her overly spent, and she feels it *now* in her chest.

Forcing the wind and snow to stay away is like stopping a landslide with nothing but her bare hands. Nialla can only hope her little moments of control are enough to hold the rest of the world at bay. Like stretching a muscle, it takes work to build strength. But she did it to make it less of a struggle for her parents.

Sackery always warns her of the consequences of upsetting the natural balance surrounding them.

But she doesn't see what's wrong with bending a few branches to clear a path.

Nialla walks among the graves outside the tomb. Most of the names on the stone monuments have worn off, but she can read a few of the words written in her mother's tongue. After a while, the old man and her mother join her with their things packed, and they begin looking for a way down the mountains.

They walk into canyons steeper than an abyss, the snow up to their knees.

Undoubtedly, the Vedrethal and her mother are left to trudge through the worst. Nialla climbs atop the rocks, allowing her to steal their path with the lightest steps. Sackery laughs as he watches her jump from an outcropping to an icy bridge, never slipping on a landing. Nialla couldn't care less about how deep the snow is or how hard the wind blows.

After a couple of days, the trio discovers the remnants of wayshrines along their road, stacks of rocks with writings etches into the face of the larger stones.

Sackery decides to camp next to these shrines a few times, the snow behind them.

On these nights, when the sky's clear and wolves howl, the three sit quietly to enjoy the calm. Sometimes, they go a few days without saying a word. Sometimes, a few weeks. After journeying together for so many years, Nialla relishes the occasions she feels alone. She looks out to the stars, wondering what they are until her mother catches her awake and tells her to sleep.

Then the mornings come, and the three push on until their legs need to stop again.

Sackery notices a new mountain range breaking the southern horizon.

"Lurhan," Cyridel utters.

"The lands of the Ellúndar. Your people," Sackery describes as if repeating it from an old song.

"No. Only my kindred, not my people," Cyridel faithfully corrects him. Nialla notices her squint as she looks further. "Invala Dailn sits behind those mountains, somewhere. But can you see that in the valley below them? Over there." She points at the ridgeline.

Nialla leans forward and peers.

"I don't see anything but a large stretch of land," Sackery returns.

He nudges Nialla's shoulder as if asking her if she can see the same as her mother.

Nialla's head pains as a ringing dulls her ears.

She twists her neck and beats her shoulders back, clenching her fist as she tries to throw it out of her mind. Within the noise, she can hear a voice . . . or . . . voices, speaking to her like a hammer to her skull. An image of a *monster* lunges at her, the clouds turning black on red. Nialla closes her eyes and covers her ears, wanting to scream, only to find she can't make a sound. All she can do is listen to the words as the world around her darkens:

"Áeiltheram . . . Áeiltheram . . . Áeiltheram!"

She's on the ground next, curled into a ball, Sackery having thrown his cloak over her.

Nialla's nose bleeds, and a bulge in her throat causes her to gasp for air.

"She's awake!" Sackery shouts.

"Nialla?" her mother asks.

"I am okay," Nialla breathes. "What happened?"

"You collapsed," Sackery explains.

"Look at her! She's as pale as snow," her mother says.

"She needs heat," Sackery instructs.

Nialla wrings her palms. Her fingers are . . . numb. Is this what the cold feels like?

Sackery lights a fire and carries Nialla over to it. He wraps every blanket they have around her shoulders, rubbing her hands together.

"It's okay . . . You're fine," he tells her. "We almost thought you died."

"I felt like I wanted to," Nialla shudders.

"What happened?"

"I don't . . . I don't know."

"But you *do* know."

"Was it another waking nightmare?" Cyridel asks, folding her hands in her lap.

"Nightmare? No. She didn't blow out the side of the mountain," Sackery denies. "This was different."

Nialla's mother hurries to her pack and takes out a bundle of leaves wrapped in waxy paper. She plucks a fresh one stuffed into the center and holds it out. "This should help."

"What is it," Nialla warily asks.

"A weed I collect as we go," Cyridel kindly smiles. "But I should warn you, it'll taste like rotten wood." She kneels next to her and rests a hand on Nialla's chest. "Tilt your head back and open your mouth. Can you swallow? There we go. Good."

Nialla nearly gags as she fights to put it down.

"Better?" Sackery asks.

"No," Nialla coughs.

"You'll be all right," he sighs. "Now tell us what happened."

"I don't know," Nialla tells him again.

"You *do* know," Sackery urges.

Her mother puts a hand on the Vedrethal's arm.

Sackery looks at her and frowns, nodding as he turns back with water in his eyes.

"Did you see or feel anything?" her mother asks. "Anything at all?"

"I saw a—?" Nialla shudders. "A three-headed crow with six wings. Maybe?"

Sackery crosses his arms. "A crow?"

"With three heads."

"And six wings," Sackery iterates.

"What does that even mean?" Cyridel asks.

"I don't know," Sackery admits.

"It felt like I was under attack," Nialla recites. "But they were far . . . far away . . . but they could see me, somehow."

Sackery tugs at the edges of the blankets covering her. "An oppressive force? Like a shade in the shape of a crow," he weighs, stopping to think. "Are you sure? I've never known such a creature. And I fought most of them."

"She's never had a wrong feeling before," Cyridel points out.

"Never is a strong word," Sackery cautions.

"And *it* spoke to me," Nialla shudders.

"Spoke to you? How—?"

Sackery draws back and puts his thumb to his lips as if suddenly disturbed.

"Like three voices speaking as one," Nialla describes. "I . . . didn't know the word."

"Could you tell if what it said was a threat?" Sackery asks.

"How am I supposed to know that?" Nialla begs the question.

"Ais emón manüra. Behn dríl amoír laúel," her mother whispers in her native tongue. "Can you remember? Speak it if you can."

"Áeiltheram," Nialla mutters hardly above a whisper.

She watches as Sackery's eyes widen when Nialla says the word. He closes his mouth and kneels beside her, shaking his head as if he had just heard a ghost.

"Áeiltheram? I may not understand Aarendelic well," Sackery admits, "but I know *that* tongue."

"You recognize it?" Cyridel asks.

"Of a kind," Sackery shifts. "Iírdun. Spoken by Old Eedian."

Nialla sits up as she hears the name.

"Vedreron," her mother evokes.

"It's her father's tongue," Sackery clarifies. "Mostly only spoken by survivors like me."

"Or those with close ties to those days. What does it mean?"

"Welcome," Nialla realizes.

Sackery looks at her and nods. "I don't like it."

Nialla throws off the blankets and stands up, walking to the path's edge to look over the valley under the distant mountains. She counts the many rivers swimming across the landscape, cutting through the vast forests and open prairies of yellow grass.

"Somebody bids us a welcome home," Nialla whispers.

"Or warning us to stay away," Sackery alludes.

"Do you know this place?"

"That? We called it the Eskiel Valley—fertile soil fed by waters coming down the mountains," he recalls. "We'll descend and cross the River Norah east of the fork. There is a plateau with a good view over the surrounding countryside, the Greencliffs above Wilhimusk. There's a freshwater pond and some woods nearby where we can find timber. Looking for a home? I daresay we won't find better."

"Wilhimusk," Nialla repeats.

"How long will it take us to get there?" Cyridel asks.

Sackery narrows his gaze at her. "At least a month? Maybe two by our road?"

"And how close will it bring us to the Seclumor Wilds?"

Nialla watches Sackery fall back a step. "Why do you ask?" he begs the question.

"Vanhan Matsan," her mother iterates.

"Ancient Wood," Nialla whispers.

Sackery looks at her briefly and frowns. "You don't want to go?"

"No. It's not that," Cyridel shudders.

"Then what?"

"I've heard stories about those wilds."

"Every tree has a story. Why does it matter?"

"Because these Crows are not the only threat we may face," her mother cautions.

"Maithandír . . . You're afraid we might find them," Sackery realizes.

"We'd be close to their borders," Cyridel judges. "They would not be so charitable to outsiders."

"That is our road forward," Sackery presses.

"And you agreed," Nialla tells her.

She watches as her mother's eyes flutter. "I am outnumbered," Cyridel surrenders.

Nialla smiles and peels away from the view over the valley, running ahead of Sackery and her mother. The land below them sits at the edge of the known world, with mountains, rivers, grasslands, and trees to get lost in and explore. But as joy washes over Nialla, a darker aspect remains.

A steady drum rings in her ears as she moves against the

wind, haunting her steps.

Nialla stops and waits at the start of a bend in the road, the weight of the shadow pressing on her shoulders.

She breathes in and holds it, closing her eyes while letting her air out slowly.

"I don't care what you are," Nialla tells it. "Get out of my head."

And the beating stops, almost as if it were suddenly in awe.

— 4 —

TO WALK AMONG THEM

They spend weeks following the hidden roads down the mountains. It was hard to descend the snowcapped peaks against the winds, but they finally did after a month. Sackery now hums, building castles in the sky to keep his mind busy on the long trek.

When they touch the soil of the fertile crescent of the Eskiel Valley, the Daughter of Ilhivendal looks up. She says: "Arún Ouandin," in a warm, confident tone. Nialla and Sackery glance at her with awe-struck wonder. "In case you forgot what the Sydaunaen called those lands."

"I never forgot," Sackery says. "Their descendants built Invala Dailn."

"And eventually became the Maithandír and Míran," Cyridel murmurs. "Ellúndar."

Sackery takes Nialla by the hand and keeps moving forward. They cross a field with grass nearly as tall as Cyridel. The woman stays back momentarily before following their footsteps, cutting a swath through the meadow. Just another field in another land, no different than the last hundred they walked. But this place has a history that even the Storyteller of Ilhivendal wouldn't recall. And the old man lived through most of it, which is telling.

The nature of the Ellúndar is that of Cyridel's lost kin. Like her, they can live for centuries, but their memories only go back so far. Cyridel is young for her kind, barely more than a child, but older than three generations of men. It reminds Sackery of some words his adopted father once told him:

"Eternal life fades away the longer you endure it," Icurian said. "And you can *only* endure it. Yesterday is a blur. Don't be a man to remain in the past, but remember, you can't escape it, either. Let these stories guide your hands." A shiver crawls down Sackery's neck as the voice whispers in his ear again.

After three more days of traveling south, the trio crosses the remnants of an old battlefield, mostly grown over by moss and grass. Sackery finds the skeletal remains of warriors scattered across a maze of rocks.

"This was the initial clash, the frontline," Cyridel points as she paces along the boulders. "Soldiers of the Maithandír . . . Hundreds. Notice the threads on their banners? Yellow and black."

Sackery looks, but he can hardly tell the cloth from the rot. "Not much survived," he notions.

"I don't see much other than dust and bone," Nialla agrees.

"How long ago, do you think?" Cyridel asks him.

Sackery runs a hand over deep scars in the dirt, untouched by time. "A thousand years? Maybe fewer."

"And how can you guess that?" Nialla asks.

"Because this wasn't here last time I traveled this road," Sackery tells the girl.

Nialla squints at him before letting off a frown. She kneels by one of the bodies, or what's left of it. The girl hovers a hand over the face of the skull, closing her eyes and muttering to herself. Sackery wonders if she can see what happened here—right now—like another waking nightmare.

Cyridel lets out a soft lament. "Fractious. That's how my father described the old kingdom," she elucidates. "Or what little he could tell me. Perhaps they—?"

Sackery shakes his head. He comes across more bodies, all left where they died, their heads crushed, their armor shattered at the breastplate.

"This wasn't a war," he interposes. "It was a slaughter. One-sided."

"You can tell that? How?"

"Do you see how the bodies lay?" Sackery motions. "All in the same direction."

Cyridel looks at him from a few steps away, a tremor to her lips. "We shouldn't stay here."

"Can we move on?" Nialla willfully asks.

Sackery looks at the girl and notices a tremor in her shoulders. Is she cold? After their trek through the mountains, he questions if that's possible.

They walk the battleground, looking for a way through without disturbing the dead.

"Where are we?" Cyridel asks.

"At the bottom of the valley," Sackery tells them. "There should be a river south of us. We'll ford and press westward until we reach Trebunor—an old sprawl at the edge of the Maithandír lands. And if I were to guess, these soldiers came from there."

"Which doesn't bode well for the city since last time you passed this way," Cyridel suggests.

"It doesn't make sense," Sackery frowns, pressing his palms together.

"What doesn't?" Nialla asks.

He scoops up a fistful of dirt and lets it drain through his fingers. "King Herranol wouldn't have surrendered this valley without cause. He's not one to let threats go unanswered. Morenarch never made it past the Klashmere Mountains, and the Morkül never marched this far south. So, what killed these troops?" Sackery mostly asks under a whisper, letting the idea linger in the air.

"Maybe he died here?"

"No. I doubt that very much," Sackery rejects.

"Then what?" Cyridel questions.

"I don't know," he admits. "Maybe they withdrew to Invala Dailn?"

"And left these soldiers behind?"

"Would that surprise you? Holding the line is hard when half your kinfolk abandons you."

"You're saying my grandfather did *this* when he led the Long March?"

"No. But every action has a consequence. Sometimes, it takes longer for us to see our mistakes."

"Only for it to be too late when we finally do?" Cyridel begs the question.

"I understand that history thrives on making fools out of the wisest men," Sackery admits. "Come. Let's move on."

They proceed down to the river and follow the north bank until they reach a track for them to cross. Sackery tosses a rock into the water, only to watch it disappear under the fast-moving surface.

"Deeper than it looks," he says, feeling his throat.

"Do I have to swim that?" Nialla asks.

"It's only a short way," the girl's mother says.

Nialla looks at the water and swallows. Afraid. She grew up on stories of how her father killed the dragon Morenarch by drowning it in the Arudenbay. But at the cost of his own life. Taherian Endúcar fell when the bridge collapsed from under him, taking the dragon with him into the waters below the cliffs at Calidor.

Stories like that can easily make the bravest souls wary of the simplest things.

"It's all right," Sackery comforts her. "Do you want me to

carry you?" He kneels to Nialla and offers her a hand.

Nialla frowns, nodding and accepting it. "Thank you," she murmurs.

Sackery picks the girl up and places her on his shoulders, letting her wrap her arms around his head.

"One day soon, I won't be around to be the bridge you need, little one," he tells her. "And a little water will seem so small when the true challenges of the world show themselves."

"You're not afraid of when it rains," Cyridel quietly laughs. "That's made of water."

Nialla shudders. "It's not the water." She tightens her grip on Sackery as he wades into the riverbank. "I don't want to drown."

"It's only a dip," Sackery reassures her. "Once across, we're safe. Do you trust me?"

Nialla's grasp loosens. "I do. I trust you."

Cyridel grabs his arm as they push against the water, working together to keep themselves from getting swept off their feet. On the other side, Nialla jumps off him, dropping onto the dirty sand. Sackery slumps over the rocks, muscles sore and out of breath.

Both the girls lay down next to him, mud soaking their clothes.

"One thing I'll look forward to," Cyridel breathes, "is never going through another fording."

"This from a woman who grew up in a city so fond of its rivers," Sackery mocks her.

"We had bridges," Cyridel tells him. "And the waters were always clear."

"Fresh from the snows melting off the mountains," Sackery laughs.

"Not like the filth that flows here," Cyridel frowns, squeezing the end of her sleeve.

The mud coming off is grey and thick, not like dirt, but rather . . . ash. And it's everywhere. It cakes the shore like a thick sludge on the rocks. More of it covers the trees farther along the embankment, taken by the wind and the rain. The carcasses of animals—dear and birds—litter the riverside, some more fresh than others.

Sackery pushes off the ground and staggers to find his balance. His fingers draw toward the hilt of his sword, a dryness tickling the back of his throat.

Cyridel follows beside him, with Nialla inching ahead.

"First, a battlefield," she whispers. "And now this? So much death."

"A fire must've torn through here recently," Nialla suggests. "All this ash?"

"No. It's like a fine dust now," Sackery denies. "This is old. Maybe as old as those bodies across the river."

"The rains would've washed it away if it were," Cyridel notions.

"Unless it stained everything it touched," Nialla shudders.

Sackery looks to the trees and points. "Maybe. But there's a trail. See it?"

"And where does it lead?" Cyridel asks.

"Trebunor," Sackery tells her. "It's not a large city, but . . . It's shelter."

"And to Wilhimusk after that?" Nialla asks.

"If we follow the river long enough, we'll get there," Sackery admits. "Don't worry."

But then, he notices the girl tremble again. He hears a distant crack of thunder, so he looks up to see the clouds gathering on the horizon.

"Speaking of the rain?" Cyridel cocks an eyebrow.

"Almost like it's chasing us," Sackery frowns.

"How soon before it hits?" Nialla begs the question.

"Depends on how quickly we can pick up our feet," Sackery tells her.

Cyridel pulls the girl close and squeezes her shoulders. "Best to leave the weather to do what the weather does."

"Lest it comes back angrier than before," Sackery cautions, taking the lead into the wooded path.

"But I like the rain," Nialla says.

"We know you do," Cyridel returns. "And these storms *like* you, too."

"A bit too much," Sackery murmurs.

Following the trail, it widens into a paved stone road. Torrents of ash dance in the crevices, sometimes making the path hard to spot. Only the markers along the wayside keep them from wandering off, with the trees getting larger the deeper they head into the wildwood.

The clouds hang above them now, with the air heavy with the smell of wet earth. It's nearly dark, and the coming storm makes it darker.

As the rain pitters around them, Sackery stops to get his bearings at another marker, a once solid chunk of rock shattered into pieces. A struggle?

Cyridel stares at it while Nialla runs a finger along the sharp edges, where the stone broke apart.

"A battlefield? Ash in the river," Cyridel lists. "Doesn't this look like—?"

"It does," Sackery tells her.

Cyridel breathes, and it comes out as a misty cloud. "Let's find a hole for the night," the woman decides.

Sackery picks up one of the shards no larger than his thumb. "You'll have no arguments from me," he agrees, feeling the weight of the rock in his palm. "Stay close and don't lose the road." He stacks the rocky piece atop the rubble, leaving his mark, bemused at the idea that it is probably as old as him.

"And if we *do* lose our way?" Nialla asks.

"Then I'll come find you," Sackery tells her flatly.

"No matter what?"

Sackery turns and smiles: "No matter what," he promises.

— 5 —

THE KEEPER

"There's a light ahead!" Sackery calls back.

Cyridel looks up from under her hood. "Where?" she asks.

The deluge covets the old forest road, making the trek slippery with mud. "In the trees!" the Vedrethal shouts. "Do you see it?" But she sees nothing but the branches flying in the wind and water blasting into her face. Cyridel wipes her eyes and looks again, taking Nialla's hand as she spots a soft glow between the leaves.

"What is that?" she asks.

"A beacon? Or a fire," Sackery weighs the likelihood. "It's hard to tell, but it's high."

"Above us? On a hill?" Nialla asks.

"No. More likely a tower," Sackery tells the girl. "This is the city's outskirts."

"Trebunor," Cyridel murmurs.

Sackery nods, but she can hardly tell in the wet dark. Together, they push on, coming to a bend in the road and meeting the gatehouse of a forgotten city. Thunder roars, and the three find cover in what appears to be an old horse stable, with one side collapsed and the roof half-eaten by time.

Cyridel stops in a damp corner as Sackery takes Nialla aside to wrap her in his cloak.

"We can stay here tonight," Sackery decides.

"And head into the city proper tomorrow?" Cyridel asks.

"That's my hope," the other agrees.

Cyridel presses her hand on the wall and runs her fingers across the intricate etchings in the stone and rotten woodwork. Under the moss and the ash, there's beauty here, no doubt. Trebunor, like Ilhivendal, is a kingdom-city, most likely settled by the Maithandír of Invala Dailn as a bridge between their lands and the outside. But she doesn't know for certain.

Nestling in for the night, Cyridel finds a spot away from the rain leaking into the dwelling. It's not dry like a proper refuge, but it's the best they can hope for.

Nialla joins her, laying her head on Cyridel's lap and quickly falling asleep.

Cyridel listens to her daughter's breaths, slow and steady but deeper with every inhale.

She brushes a few stray hairs behind the child's ear, humming a lullaby to keep the nightmares away.

Sackery guards the entry to the stables, where the wall collapsed, ignoring the mist as it sweeps into the shelter. Cyridel glances at him as he leans against a pillar, his arms crossed, the grey of his hood covering his eyes. She can only see the bottom of his mouth and the tip of his nose, but she can tell his focus is on the road outside.

Cyridel wipes the mud off her cloak and pulls it to her neck to ward off the dampness.

"Afraid something will attack us in the dark?" she asks him. "We aren't in the mountains anymore."

"No," Sackery concedes. "But these woods have their share of dangers."

"How long are we going to do this?"

"Not for much longer."

"Wilhimusk?"

"It's our home. We only need to get there."

"And what is *home* to you? Really?"

Sackery turns his head to her and frowns. "Someplace that draws you to it," he details.

"Like a feeling?"

"An instinct? More than a feeling," Sackery clarifies. "My kind made a choice when we left Islinin. Icurian wanted us to serve our roles as protectors—warriors, scholars, and historians. We took after the Vedreron and became their Vedrethal. The rest founded a kingdom in the north and lost everything."

"And those others became the Aens," Cyridel describes.

"Aenümorian? That's the name they call themselves now,"

Sackery explains. "Lúcran's folk. A race of men born of two worlds. Humanity before they found their heart and the Vinvidur Fólk before they drowned themselves to save their future. I was a boy at the time. Ancient history."

"You never had a home," Cyridel understands.

"Icurian raised me," Sackery admits. "No matter his crimes after, I am grateful to him."

"Why did he change?" Cyridel asks.

"That very question nearly tore the world apart," Sackery mourns. "One day, like any other, Icurian decided to go east over land . . . As far east as east will go until becoming west. Another road to Islinin. After the fall of Géurdinhal, there were no safe harbors on the continent. He didn't want the dragons to know he'd come."

"My Galron said he was looking for someone?" Cyridel mentions.

"All he told me was that he left something behind," Sackery tells her. "I thought he went searching for the Vinvidur Fólk. And I still think that, but it wasn't his only reason." The Vedrethal smiles down at Nialla asleep in Cyridel's lap, a heaviness to the girl's breath to match the storm. "It left me with questions I still don't have answers for."

He squeezes his wrist before looking away.

Cyridel understands when the Vedrethal no longer wants to talk on a subject. She puts her head down and closes her eyes, hoping to let her mind wander to a better time when they weren't always on the road, living in the ruins of civilization.

As she wakes up, a dense fog has taken over the air. Cyridel can barely see her hand in front of her nose.

Nialla is nowhere in the old stables. Nor is Sackery guarding the door by the collapsed wall.

Cyridel pushes off the ground and staggers, catching herself on a broken gate hanging by the hinge.

She wanders outside. "Sackery? Nialla?! Where are you two?" she asks the big empty.

Not even the birds answer her . . . There are *no* birds, except maybe the crows laughing in the trees. Cyridel flinches, not expecting them. It is an unpleasant noise to hear after waking up in a place she doesn't know. Why is it abandoned? Everything smells like . . . musk, but with rot lingering underneath.

She looks up at the light through the trees and the fog—a soft glow high on some precipice farther along the road.

Sackery and Nialla must've gone toward it while she slept. That, or *this*, all of it, is a dream, and she's yet to wake from it.

Cyridel walks around the bend and loses her breath, for through the haze, she can tell that in front of her, Trebunor stands. Great bastions line the streets as a high fortress commands the cliffside where the river forks. Most of the city is downtrodden and, as best Cyridel can see, in ruins, much like the stables they took shelter in for the night.

"Nialla!" Sackery calls over the thick air. "Nialla! Where are you?!"

"Sackery?!" Cyridel shouts back. "Can you hear me?" She crosses over a small footbridge and into the city proper.

"Cyridel?" Sackery begs the question. "What are you—?" He approaches her in an alleyway, but his face is a blur in the dark.

"Where's my daughter?" Cyridel demands.

"She walked off during the night."

"I got that. But why?"

"I don't know, but I chased after her! Lost her in this murk."

"She couldn't have gotten far."

"These ruins are a maze."

"Then we follow the light. The beacon . . . Where is it?"

Sackery points to the northernmost tower. "There! At least, the best I can see from here."

"It seems the most likely place she'd head to. But how do we get there?"

"There's a road that leads through," Sackery instructs. "Past the courtyard."

"After you," Cyridel motions. "I'll follow."

"Watch your step," Sackery warns. "This place is unstable. Most of these buildings are about to fall."

"Just be sure not to stand under them when they do," Cyridel advises.

"I will keep that in mind," the man chuckles.

They march to the tower on the far side of Trebunor, walking over the ancient stonework and decaying parapets. The soldiers who once patrolled these low streets are likely dead in the field they passed on their way to the city. Victims.

"How many lived here?" Cyridel whispers.

"A few hundred families," Sackery notions. "Likely with a small garrison."

Cyridel swears she can hear children playing in the fountains that dot the path. When they reach the base of the tower, she turns her eyes to its crest, able to see the muted glow of the beacon bouncing off the stonework. Stepping through the threshold of the entry, Sackery leads her up the stairwell.

"Nialla!" she calls out.

"I am here," the girl answers from somewhere.

Sackery looks at Cyridel with a frown. "She's above us," he says, climbing the remaining stairs.

Cyridel stops at a tower window overlooking much of the city. The fog dissipates through the ruined Trebunor like water flowing between rocks in a stream, with the sun peaking over the valley fields, a cold warmth that struggles to find its way through the hills. And for a second, it blinds her to what's underneath.

"Are you okay?" Sackery nudges her.

She turns to him, feeling her stomach churn.

"Everything's quiet," Cyridel murmurs. "Even the wind."

"The worst went by us overnight," Sackery tells her.

"And what if the world realizes there's more yet to come?" she asks.

Sackery falls back a step. "I don't understand."

"It doesn't matter. Nialla. Where is she?"

"Just a little farther. Come on."

They discover Nialla sitting at the top of the stairs, peeking over the ledge.

Cyridel touches her daughter's shoulder, careful not to startle her. The girl briefly looks at her before returning her attention, the glow of the beacon fire kindling her face. "Nialla? Why did you—?"

"There's a man," she utters.

"A man?" Cyridel asks.

"By the beacon fire, slumped over," Nialla tells her. "He looks . . . dead? Or he *should* be."

Cyridel glances over the ledge to see a man sitting limp by the fire near the tower's central dais—head folded into his knees, almost like the stranger is crying. He's not dead. Not yet, but he surely looks like a corpse, sobbing in his loneliness. Old and ragged.

Sackery sneaks beside them. "Be careful," he whispers. "We don't know—"

Nialla jumps to her feet and moves toward the stranger. Cyridel grabs after her, but the girl shrugs her off and steps onto the dais.

"Who's there?" the old man demands, lifting his head. "Is somebody coming? No! It's another trick. Fingertips plucking at the heartstrings? They will not fool me again! Must not. I want—" His tone peaks and shunts with every syllable, the wary ramblings of a lunatic afraid to pull himself out of a dream.

"It's all right," Nialla hushes. "We're real. Don't be afraid."

The stranger looks at her and blinks wildly, peeking out from under his tattered hood, though only briefly. He quickly ducks back inside before muttering in Aarendelic . . . Aarendelic . . . Her mother's tongue. "Shérit emón déshre, ahranok ela bleo'de," he prattles. Cyridel walks to him and listens. *She's there, flesh and blood.*

"You're one of the Maithandír," Cyridel realizes.

"A survivor?" Sackery asks.

"Look at him," Nialla mourns. "He hasn't survived."

The girl moves closer to the man, her hand held out like she would if approaching a wild cat.

"Nialla?" Cyridel asks. "What are you doing?"

"He's lost. Don't you feel it?" Nialla begs the question.

"All I can feel is that he doesn't quite know where he is," Cyridel warns.

"Which means he's dangerous," Sackery agrees.

"Dangerous? Yes. They are," the man prattles. "Always there! Always watching in the shadows of the trees."

"They?" Cyridel asks.

"Crows! Never *not* the Crows!" the man sobs.

Sackery moves between them, his fingers on his sword hilt. "What's your name?" he demands.

"Name? No names . . . Names are bad! We are only beasts. All we are . . . meat suits, puppets filled with sand. But you've arrived! At last," the man shouts. "Herranol? He didn't forget his promise! The king never forgets. Nor does he forgive. He promised to send us aid, and here you are! The last defenders lost faith and ran into the wilds, seeking salvation from the dark. They took them, one by one, until only a few were left. Me? You! All of us."

"Nobody sent us," Cyridel refuses him.

"He's more than lost," Sackery warns her.

Cyridel turns to him with a heaviness to her brows. She decides to step around the Vedrethal and toward the broken man. Sackery attempts to stop her, but all Cyridel does is shake her head, and the warrior lets her through.

"Who are you?" she asks.

The other's lips twist confusingly. "Do you not already know?" the stranger begs the question, a pride showing through his eyes. "I am the last . . . A sentry who guards the tower, a soldier on the walls. The only one to remain. They called me . . . What did they call me? Ah, Yeavengeritt! That was the name, wasn't it?"

"Yeavengeritt," Nialla mutters.

A crack dominates the air as the girl speaks the name.

Yeavengeritt stares darkly at Nialla, a tremor in his hands as if looking at her causes him no small amount of pain.

Cyridel sees hints of a man under the dirt on his face, but very little bleeds through.

"My name . . . I remember it now. Why did I forget? I used to speak it as a reminder . . . Yeavengeritt . . . Yeavengeritt . . . Yeavengeritt . . . Just like that! Yes. Years passed, and I began doubting whether help would arrive. Herranol told us he would, then nobody came."

There's an alarming melody inside this man . . . Cyridel reels back, a tingling in her throat. For years, she's become familiar with seeing the suffering in others. Life always finds newer and crueler ways to toy with those left vulnerable by conflict. Yet this is . . . different. Yeavengeritt is unwell, even for a man wallowing in the dark such as him. Something's driven him to this state.

"You're all right. Yeavengeritt, is it? We're here now." Cyridel levels with the odd creature. "How about you come with us? We've got some food and blankets. Good company? That's if you find a brooding old soldier and a young girl avid conversationalists."

Sackery narrows her eyes at her, less than amused. He shrugs all the same.

"I am Sackery Greywolfe," he introduces.

"Greywolfe? I know that name," Yeavengeritt muses. "Sackery of the Vedrethal."

"Yes. How do you—?"

"Some names you don't forget," the man issues. "Old names. Dangerous names like yours."

"I am Cyridel Elendsah. And Nialla, my daughter," Cyridel offers.

"You? You are not Maithandír," Yeavengeritt reads her. "Not for a long time. You have an accent."

"I am from the north," Cyridel explains.

"Ellúndar shouldn't live in the north," the other denies. "Those who left us never returned. No word. Galronallin led them to die."

Cyridel takes a step back and shoves her anger into her stomach.

"We didn't die," she tells him. "You don't know what you're talking about."

Sackery touches her arm. "Don't do this. Not here," he warns her.

"Why not?"

"Look at him. There's nothing left."

"He survived long enough," Cyridel utters.

"Survived with *the Crows* and the worms," Yeavengeritt rambles. "Not what you'd call a life." The man pushes to his feet but collapses right away. "They're watching . . . Always watching me, this place . . . All the birds in the trees? They listen as I sleep and when I shit in the woods. You can always tell when they play their games. They sing to me! I hate their music."

"We shouldn't leave him," Nialla urges, circling the tower.

"And what would you have us do, Nells? Take him with us?" Sackery asks.

"We can help him," she pushes.

"Nialla? No, it's—?"

"Dangerous? What isn't?" the girl argues.

"He's a lost soul that would've done better to have died years ago," Sackery explains.

"A shadow of a remnant," Yeavengeritt speaks.

Cyridel looks under the man's hood and the tears in his eyes. "How long has it been since you had a change of clothes? Come on. We're taking you down from here. Let's clear your head with some fresh air."

"Clear my head? No, no, no . . . Not with *them* lurking elsewhere."

She turns to the empty tower. "Them? Nobody else is here." Cyridel lowers a hand to the poor man. Yeavengeritt doesn't take it. He's too afraid. And that fear blazes in his eyes as she leans closer to the madman, wanting to soothe him. "Let us help you! Why stay in this place?"

Yeavengeritt's face twitches as he refuses to answer . . . Or can't. Instead, he pulls his cloak over his head, wanting to hide.

"Please leave," the sad creature pleads. "And don't come back. Leave before *the Crows* see you." His voice wanes to a whisper, difficult to hear.

Cyridel doesn't know what else to do. She stands over the Maithandír of a man, speechless. He must have once been a proud soldier fighting for Trebunor—a guard on the walls— but now? There's so little left of him inside, only the husk the man's become.

She turns to leave when she notices Nialla looking at her from across the dais.

"You can't help this man," Cyridel tells her daughter. "He doesn't want it."

"His mind's broken," Sackery iterates. "It's lapsing somewhere between clarity and utter ruin."

Nialla shakes her head. "What's broken can be fixed," the girl says. Her voice brightens the air in the tower enough to cause the beacon fire to grow. "Wounds can heal when given a chance. Sackery? You taught me that. As did you." Her stare hits Cyridel unblinkingly.

"Some wounds don't heal," Sackery explains. "Sometimes, it doesn't matter how long they rest."

"That's not fair," Nialla mourns.

"That's the way life is," Cyridel agrees.

"A life hardly worth the cost of pebbles in the sand," Yeavengeritt admits. "Water in a creek, always rushing to its end."

Nialla steps toward him, walking past her mother.

Cyridel attempts to catch her daughter's shoulder, but Nialla doesn't stop.

"No. Stay away from me!" Yeavengeritt cries. Nialla does not heed him. One foot after another, ignoring his pleas. "Please don't. They will hurt us if you—" But he doesn't get to finish what he wants to say.

Nialla whispers forcefully. "Listen to my song now."

She presses her fingertips against the man's cheeks, laying her forehead against his. Yeavengeritt sobs. He twists and curls until he finally breaks into a panic. Nialla clenches him tighter as he tries to push her away, but the girl is stronger than she looks. Or *he* is weaker, his muscles barely able to keep him sitting upright.

"Please don't," Yeavengeritt appeals. "They will peel our flesh from our bones, laughing all the while as we scream."

"I am not afraid of a few birds," Nialla fights his resistance.

Cyridel moves to see her daughter's face as the air becomes colder than it was in the mountains. The blue of her hood fades to a stark white, and the color of the morning sky turns grey. And with it, the air tastes bitter, like a winter breeze shoving itself against her.

"That's enough!" Cyridel shouts. "Nialla? No more."

She rushes forward, grabbing the girl by her wrists and pulling her away from the man.

Sackery runs to catch the girl before she hits the ground. Nialla coughs heavily in his arms. Her nose bleeds, but the Vedrethal wipes it away with his sleeve.

"It's all right," Sackery comforts. "You're okay. Follow my voice."

"Sackery?" Cyridel asks.

"She's unconscious."

"Exhausted?"

"More like drunk," he admits.

Cyridel drops to the ground and frowns. "How?" she asks.

"She must've pulled in whatever life she could to feed the man," Sackery explains. He glowers at the stranger beside him, hunched over, his head folded into his arms like a toddler trying to hide in plain sight. "Which leaves the question—?"

"Did it work?" Cyridel murmurs.

She inches toward the stranger of a man and lifts his chin.

Yeavengeritt . . . drops back, completely winded. He takes a moment and breathes. Cyridel reacts by anchoring the man as he pushes off the steppingstones. Yeavengeritt's muscles are so thin she's afraid he might break a bone if he gets up too fast.

"How did she—? Oh, her eyes," Yeavengeritt murmurs in a new voice. He looks at Nialla cradled in Sackery's arms, her lids fluttering quickly. "How do I know those eyes? Silver, like fountains glowing in the morning sun." His face dulls as Cyridel studies him, seeing the fear reflect off his pupils and into hers. "But perhaps it's not wise to say more here. Or anywhere, for that matter."

"What do you mean?" Sackery asks, lifting Nialla off the ground to carry her.

"Because they will hear it. And then? At their discretion, they *will* come."

Cyridel slings his arm around her shoulders, taking the brunt of his weight. "Can you walk?" she asks him.

"After a while? Once my legs find their strength," Yeavengeritt murmurs. "But why did you come?"

"Does it matter? We're here now," Sackery chides. "And with more questions than answers."

Cyridel shakes her head at the Vedrethal to discourage him from overwhelming Yeavengeritt. "Are you feeling better, at least? We've got food. It's not much, but you look like you haven't eaten for a long time." She counts the ribs popping out from under the man's threadbare cloak like a rope stretched to its breaking point.

Yeavengeritt smiles. Even in his face, his muscles strain to handle the modest effort.

"I wish I could feel better," Yeavengeritt admits. "Before, it was all a cloudy mess, and I couldn't feel how weak I was. Now? I feel everything. And it hurts."

Cyridel raises her shoulders until he's able to stand without her assistance. It's clear to her that Yeavengeritt's world is most *unclear*, and he's having difficulty focusing on what's in front of him. But, despite that, the Maithandír surrenders a peaceful look, absent of the madman's ramblings.

His words are a challenge to voice, but he *is* grateful. That much Cyridel reads by the subtle tilt of his head.

"You can stay with us," Sackery offers. "We will share what we have. Just don't expect a feast."

Yeavengeritt folds his hands together. "Thank you," he says.

Sackery clenches his jaw as he carries Nialla down the tower's stairs. "Follow me," he urges.

Yeavengeritt glances at Cyridel before she encourages him to follow the old Vedrethal. It's a slow tread for the man, fighting every step so as not to fall as he moves. He grips onto the railings, plodding down one bare foot at a time.

She doesn't go with them. Not right away. Cyridel walks to the tower's edge, looking to the horizon. She can see the mountains in the distance, the rivers bending through the valley and beyond its fields and trees. But lights catch her attention nearest the hills—hundreds, like a stream on fire, following the riverbank.

It's a different road than what Sackery led them through on their way to Trebunor.

Cyridel's seen such a glow before.

"Torchlight," she whispers. "Settlers of men."

— 6 —

MANY QUESTIONS

"I don't understand," Sackery derides. "That's quite a long time to survive alone."

"Not all life abandoned Trebunor," Yeavengeritt whispers. "Some have stayed—the brave and the stupid."

Sackery leans forward, stoking their little campfire. "And which are you?" he asks Yeavengeritt.

He's not arguing that somebody can't hold out within the city, but he can't deny that everything else is dead. Staying in this place would mean the man saw no hope in leaving or was so lost in the dark that he couldn't find his way out. And neither is particularly good news for Sackery and his wards.

"Can't I be a bit of both?" Yeavengeritt answers with a question. "I did not stay by choice, Vedrethal. Every time I've tried walking past the border, I lose all sense of direction. And with it, I get this overwhelming feeling that if I step outside, bad things will happen."

Nialla wakes in the corner where Sackery had left her after carrying her back to the stables. He hands her dried jerky to munch on as breakfast.

"Bad things? That doesn't tell me much," Sackery sighs.

"It's a tinge at the back of the neck," Yeavengeritt admits. "Like when you're at the water's edge, and the tide's coming fast onto the shore."

"And every bone in your body tells you to run away," Cyridel finishes, ducking into the shelter.

Sackery frowns. Cyridel had stayed back in the tower. He had a mind to return to the city and find her, but Yeavengeritt's kept him busy with his half-baked stories, the nightmare he's lived for decades. He was a young man when Trebunor stood proud over the Eskiel Valley. But now the Maithandír is as old as the Storyteller of Ilhivendal.

And that's no short life.

"Find what you were looking for?" Sackery asks the woman.

"Only broken houses and dead things," Cyridel admits. "And I spotted, how should I say? Visitors."

"More visitors?" Yeavengeritt repeats, looseness in his tone.

"Where?" Sackery demands.

"Coming up the river valley," Cyridel explains. "Settlers. Most likely men, looking for land to claim."

"After decades, the chain finds another loop," Sackery mutters. "How far are they?"

"Three days? Maybe less," Cyridel says, squeezing her

wrists.

Sackery buries his face into his palms. They spent all these years escaping civilization, all to protect the girl from what society would do if they discovered *who* and *what* she was . . . But it seems that life has caught up to them, and they've run out of road to stay out of its way.

Cyridel languishes just inside the door, the sunlight breaking through the roof. Sackery looks at her, waiting for her to tell him they should leave. But she doesn't.

"We can't keep running," Nialla urges. "I say we wait for them. Ask what they want."

"But the question is, are we *safe* if we stay?" Cyridel murmurs.

The old horse stable darkens as the four mull over the word silently. "Safe," Sackery scoffs.

Safe. What does that mean these days? He doesn't know. But he *knows* that *fear* prevalent in Yeavengeritt's eye, as clear as the fire between them.

"Should you stay, *the Crows* will come," the Maithandír warns. "And if they come, nowhere will be safe."

"Crows again? You spoke of them in the tower," Cyridel denotes. "You aren't talking about the birds, are you?"

Yeavengeritt grimly shakes his head.

"You believe these Crows are what keep you here?" Sackery demands.

"It takes a sane man to know when he loses his wits!" the man defends. The anguish in his eyes subsides by a fresh rawness, only for him to catch himself and draw back where he sits. "I am sorry. You don't deserve that tone, Vedrethal." He looks at Nialla. The girl meets his gaze and offers him a kindly smile. "I only want you to understand."

Sackery reaches for Nialla and lays a hand on her back. "It's okay," he tells them both, lowering his voice to sound more tenderly.

"We saw a depiction on the road," Cyridel explains. "A crow with three heads and six wings. Does that sound familiar?"

"A symbol?"

"More like a sigil," Sackery iterates.

"Or a warning," Nialla suggests.

"And a warning it would be," Yeavengeritt agrees. "Everybody hates crows and snakes."

Sackery frowns as he attempts to take the man's hand, but the Maithandír sinks away and hides under the blanket they gave him. Cyridel steps back and leans against the broken entryway, arms folded under her cloak as she looks at the wilds outside. Sackery squeezes Nialla's knee and musters to his feet.

"What do you want to do?" Sackery asks her. "Stay or go?"

"I don't know," Cyridel admits.

"Then answer me this," he notions. "Friend or foe? These men on their way?"

"It's a long way to come for unclaimed land," she realizes.

"They could be like us," Sackery offers. "Running as far away as possible, hoping nobody finds them."

"Three days," Cyridel suggests.

"Three days," he repeats.

"I don't think our new friend is well enough to travel anyway," she warns, turning to Yeavengeritt. "He's so thin. And if what he says is true?"

"That every time he wants to leave, something drags him back?" Sackery paraphrases.

"He said it differently, but yes," she agrees. "That worries me, these Crows. What could they be?"

"A folk tale? Something the locals used to scare children away from the woods?"

"But so engrained that it manifests in the real world?"

"Anything's possible. The world is mysterious, with more wonder than most can remember."

"That's why we have stories," Cyridel laughs. "To remind us."

"What better way? But after everything we survived, does a fairy tale scare you?"

"It's not for *me* that I am scared," Cyridel admits, glancing at Nialla before stepping out of the building. Sackery follows her into the trees, the ground still damp from the rain, a cold breeze sweeping over them. "We've traveled over grasslands and mountains, only to find ourselves in the woods again, faced with a dead city."

"And still a distance to go until we reach Wilhimusk," Sackery weighs.

"Three days? Are we willing to wait that long to see what

happens?" Cyridel asks.

"Nialla is," he explains. "She's the whole reason why we do any of this."

"I suppose you're right," Cyridel nods.

"And if I am not? If those men you spotted wish to settle, we can't avoid them forever," Sackery notions. "Maybe for a decade or two? But after? How do we respond if their borders reach us, and we have nowhere to go? With war? I am a soldier, but I cannot fight an army alone."

Cyridel lets off a chuckle. "Didn't you fight an army in the past?" she points out.

"With a little help from my brothers and sisters," Sackery feigns humility. "Yes. But we're alone. And I doubt Herranol would consider lending aid to a broken old Vedrethal, the lost princess of Ilhivendal, and her daughter, the last true heir to the most powerful kingdom of men in the north."

"So? We keep running?" Cyridel asks him.

"No. We build a fortress."

"As a home?"

"Is there a difference?" Sackery finishes.

The breeze comes in again, causing Cyridel's hood to fly open and show her dark, stark eyes. Sackery stares at her for a moment longer than he intends, all while she looks back at him. It isn't a look of mutual attraction but rather a quiet language. Among her lineage, the Daughter of Ilhivendal has Aenümorian blood in her veins—a gift from her mother, Nadrial Elendsah.

To the pair, a sense emanates between Cyridel and Sackery that speaks louder than words.

It is the same tickle he feels whenever Nialla meets her eyes with his, and it makes him want to cry. A tinge that's always there, lingering in his mind like a whisper that reminds him of everything he lost when he became the first of the Vedrethal.

That was the price Sackery willfully paid for the chance to serve the man who saved him and his brothers-in-arms after the war with the dragons. And since that day, he's not sure they made the right choice—a stretched life hollowed by a world wariness that no love can abate.

All he can do is keep fighting until the day comes when somebody takes his place.

— 7 —

A NEW DAWN

Cyridel waits atop the city's ramparts, watching the caravan get closer for two days.

On the third night, the riders arrive with numbers and torchlight—however, far too few for what she saw coming down the valley. The unit master calls his men to the ready as they canter across the bridge and through the lower streets, stopping at a courtyard dominated by a black, withered tree.

Cyridel becomes entranced by the flames reflecting off their cloaks and grey armor.

"As I said," Sackery glowers. "Soldiers. Not settlers."

"Should we go down and meet them?" Cyridel asks openly.

They both look at Nialla, standing at the wall's edge, hugging the black air. Cyridel leans a little forward to catch the glint in the girl's eyes, steady on the flames as the horse riders weave through the dead city's streets, disappearing behind the hollowed-out buildings. "Nells?" she nudges.

Nialla lets out a long breath. "We should," she decides.

Sackery frowns before glancing at Cyridel. "Ready?" he asks her.

"Nialla stays close to me," Cyridel agrees. "Keep our hoods up. Hide our features."

"And our new friend?" Nialla begs the question.

"Asleep. After what Yeavengeritt survived, he deserves to rest."

"We are a family from Esgrelion, traveling the old roads," Sackery tells them. "Use our common names. I am Grey-wolfe."

"And I am Miralifrim," Cyridel confirms.

"Nells," Nialla nods.

"And if they prove hostile?" Sackery asks.

"We run as fast as we can for the bridge," Cyridel recounts. "Escape into the woods."

"And head west," Nialla finishes.

"Keep the river to your right and ford at the fork," Sackery instructs. "I'll find you when I can. I promise."

Cyridel pulls her cloak over her shoulders and breathes. They work their way around to the riders, avoiding their scouts. As they move toward the central plaza, Cyridel notices the banners carried by their bearers . . . A white tower on a blue field, the flags of Calidor, the City of Towers, and the House of Endúcar.

"Maheirans?" she murmurs.

Her heart skips a beat when she spots the banners of other Noble Houses, not only from Calidor but across the north— streaks of golds and reds, greens, and sable. It is a bastard unit, most likely second or third sons and daughters of powerful lords. Their reasons? She cannot guess.

But it's not until Cyridel, Sackery, and Nialla enter the courtyard that she gets a decent view of their commander, dressed in a yellow cloak.

Many soldiers turn inward at them, stunned to find dwellers in this ruined city. They pass whispers between each other, most dismounting their horses and readying their spears. Sackery responds by laying a hand on the hilt of his sword, prepared to draw.

The commander steps between his troops and the wayward party.

He stares at them with soft eyes from under his helmet's winged-like visor. Cyridel regards the torchlight flickering on the steel, creating a dance across the commander's nose and ears. He removes his helmet and lowers it to his side.

"We didn't expect to find anyone here," the man admits, bowing his head in a cautious greeting.

Sackery returns with a nod. "Neither did we expect an army to come marching through the valley," he iterates.

The man chuckles. "Army? A few hundred fighters and their families? No. We're no army."

Cyridel relaxes her shoulders, feeling a warmth to the low-pitched tone of the commander's voice.

"Then who are you?" Sackery asks.

"Who are we? Without a doubt, we should introduce ourselves."

"A name for a name, then?"

"Rasterforn Suromount. These people call me 'lord,' but I am only a soldier. Maheiran."

"And I am Greywolfe. Warrior," Sackery cites. "This is my sister, Miralifrim, and her daughter, Nells."

Rasterforn looks at Nialla, huddled against Cyridel's side. "Daughter? And it's only you three?"

"Our great uncle travels with us, but the journey takes its toll," Cyridel explains. "He's resting in one of these buildings."

Rasterforn shakes his head. "It's not safe to journey in the wilds with so few," he says with genuine concern.

"We make do by traveling light and staying off the main roads," Sackery tells him.

"It's not the roads that scare me," Rasterforn confides.

"Afraid of the dark?" Sackery jests.

"In a matter of speaking," Rasterforn shrugs. "We've had our share of troubles."

"As have we," Cyridel smiles, pulling Nialla closer. "But we got through it. Bruised and battered, but we did."

"Then you're luckier than some," the man sighs, passing his helmet to a subordinate. "Or more skilled." Rasterforn squints at Sackery, taking stock of the warrior from his stance to his weapon. The man tilts his head in dim recognition. Under his cloak, Sackery wears the armor of the Vedrethal.

Could *that* be it?

Cyridel frowns. "Our journey from Esgrelion was a long one," she explains.

"Esgrelion?" Rasterforn repeats. "We passed through Orwynswall on our way to Rhain. Good folks."

"A strong people," Sackery agrees.

"With stronger accents," Rasterforn nods. "Accents you don't have. Which suggests you aren't from Esgrelion?"

Cyridel watches Sackery thumb his sword's pommel. "No. We're not."

"Then all is well," Rasterforn smiles, opening his arms wide. "Of course, I don't care where you're from, only that you tell me the truth. After I called you out, but still? Half of my people are refugees. So, your business isn't any of ours. We're all trespassers in this dead place. But that beacon? It's bright enough to shine halfway across this valley. We followed it for days, hoping it led to a haven."

"Trebunor," Cyridel murmurs.

"What is that?"

"This city's name. Trebunor? An old Maithandír domain on the borders of their lands."

"Maithandír? Like the Míran of Nrondon?"

"Kindred. Separated by centuries," Sackery explains.

"And . . . What did you call it? Trebunor? Powerful name," Rasterforn measures. "What happened here?"

"We don't know," Cyridel answers.

"Only that everybody left," Nialla adds.

Rasterforn smiles kindly at the girl. "Sounds ominous," he admits.

"We came across a battlefield northeast of the city," Sackery chronicles.

"My riders found a similar scene," Rasterforn agrees. "But that wasn't a battle. It was a slaughter."

"Meaning they didn't abandon it," one of the riders suggests.

"Thrown out? Most likely," Rasterforn weighs.

"But by what?" Sackery asks the question.

Rasterforn returns to his horse and plucks a leather sack from his saddle. "A question for later," the man states, offering the skin to Cyridel. "Take this. As a gesture of good faith. Honeyed wine from Arthor. A little taste of home for both of us, don't you think?"

"Honeyed wine?" Cyridel exhales, feeling the weight.

"Others call it mead. Please. As warm tidings to fellow travelers," Rasterforn says. He turns to Sackery next, sensing the man's displeasure. "You three are welcome to join our camp for as long as you want. Oh, and your 'great uncle' too, wherever he may be."

"That is very kind of you," Nialla smiles. "Thank you, Lord Rasterforn."

"Manners? Even at the edge of the world," Rasterforn laughs. "Always a surprise from the unexpected. But we live in dangerous times. And it's rare to find friendly faces, even on well-traveled roads. Don't discount the value an open hand brings." He stares at Sackery as he speaks the words.

"I never do," the Vedrethal bites, squaring his shoulders.

"Good. The rest of my caravan will likely arrive by the morn," Rasterforn says. "How long have you three—?"

"Three days," Nialla tells him.

"Three days more than mine," Rasterforn concludes. "So, if I may ask a favor?"

"You want us to show you around," Cyridel offers a guess.

"Only so we can find places to house families," Rasterforn explains. "The sooner after they arrive, the better for everybody."

"Are you planning on digging in for a siege?" Sackery asks.

Rasterforn shakes his head and frowns. "My people have come a long way, Master Greywolfe," the commander defends. "And we took losses on the hard drive south. A hundred petty kings vie for every hill and river from the northern ranges to the eastern dunes. This place can be *our* bulwark. But I want somewhere for us to sleep first."

"You care for your people," Sackery concludes. "I can respect that. And our circumstances?"

"As I said, a question for later," Rasterforn decides.

Nialla tugs Cyridel's sleeve to get her attention. "Home," she whispers.

Cyridel squeezes the girl's shoulder. "Home." The three of them step aside as Rasterforn moves by them.

Sackery pulls his hand away from his sword and crosses his arms. He doesn't break his stare as the soldiers spread out from the courtyard.

"Do you trust these men?" the Vedrethal asks once the Maheirans are out of earshot. "Tell me honestly."

Cyridel looks at him. "I didn't sense malice in his words."

"Nor do I think he lied," Nialla agrees.

"So, you think we're safe with them?" he asks.

"They'd have more to lose trusting us," Cyridel offers. "Do you see them? They're not an army."

"But they're organized," Sackery scoffs.

"Because of this 'Lord' Rasterforn," Nialla suggests. "They follow him."

"He's kept them alive through their troubles," Cyridel adds. "Just like us."

"Meaning you *want* to stay?" Sackery realizes.

Cyridel steps forward, taking Nialla by the hand. "You are the one who wants to stop running," she tells him. "This is our chance. And we can do it with *them*. They can be our *shield*, and you, their *sword*. Aren't you sick of worrying if our strength is enough to beat the challenges that come our way?"

"Maybe you're right."

"And maybe I'm not? But we can find out."

"And if it hurts us in the end? What will we lose?"

"What *can* we lose? I ran away from my home, everything I was . . . As did you."

Sackery looks at her with water in his eyes. "I can't do it again," he admits.

"Then don't," Cyridel confides. "Let's stay and help these

people. Help ourselves."

"Hope from the unexpected," Nialla offers. She speaks her father's words as if he were standing beside them.

Cyridel's heart flutters as she lets out an unsteady breath.

"That isn't fair," Sackery frowns.

"But you know she's right," Cyridel stands her ground.

Sackery drops his shoulders and looks at the tree in the courtyard. Somebody lit it on fire long ago, its branches withered, with old ash covering where its roots meet the earth. Most cities of the Ellúndar—Míran and Maithandír—have places like this, a home for the oldest trees inside their keepings.

Ilhivendal had theirs in the lowest reaches, a place Nialla's father visited often and spoke to as if it were a person.

Cyridel knows them as the weodemair trees, the lords of the forest. Always a pair, breathing life into the land to make it grow. Their roots stretch for hundreds of leagues, anchoring this world to the fabric of time and space. Alive.

But this one is dead. Was it murdered? Who killed it? The Maithandír? Or maybe the Crows in the shadows?

"We should tell Yeavengeritt," Sackery decides.

"If what he says is true—?"

"It all falls on these Crows," Sackery finishes, breaking away from the tree.

Cyridel follows him, Nialla walking alongside her. The sun now peeks over the city's walls, causing the dead weodemair's branches to reflect the light like a golden crown. Even in the darkest hours, a little warmth will always find a way.

– Rasterforn Suromount –

— 8 —

PATHS CONVERGE

She witnesses the gardens in her dreams—a virulent tide melting away into currents at her feet. Brilliant mountains stretch upward as Nialla peers at them from the valley's floor. Flower petals wither along her path, only to grow again when she touches their stems.

"Gently do the meadows become a forest all their own," Nialla recites. "They are born of light from distant stars." She pushes the dream's walls out until it joins a vast emptiness, like the clear skies above Arún. "Only for the calm shallows to wane."

It's a poem Nialla's mother sang to her on her thirtieth birthday. She'd only look like a girl of three. Now she's six years by sixty and still a child to many eyes.

Nialla sits up when she hears the horses riling.

She pushes her mother's arms away. Through the doorway,

Nialla can see the Maheirans. There's more today than there was last night. Dozens . . . hundreds . . . Rasterforn's caravan arrives in droves, with many looking exhausted. Months of hard travel on the road is difficult for anybody. She rubs her feet, knowing *that* better than most.

Rasterforn peeks in from outside, curious to see where the strangers keep themselves. But in his courtesy, he remains there, not wanting to intrude.

Sackery looks at him from the door, mending a strap he ripped during their trek over the mountains.

Nialla stands and goes to him. Rasterforn reacts in benign amusement as she approaches with all seriousness.

"I wanted to let you folks know that my people have arrived in the city," Rasterforn tells them. The sun is out, but the air's still dark, with a heavy blanket of clouds overhead. "Most of us made camp in the lower city. Near the forest bridge. My troops have taken over the palace on the cliffs."

"And how long will you stay?" Nialla asks.

Rasterforn kindly smiles. He likely meant to speak to "Greywolfe" or "Miralifrim," not the girl who is older than she appears.

"For *some* time," Rasterforn answers. "Our intention was always to build a new life. And this place, this Trebunor? Something about it catches my eye. Just don't ask me what it is." Nialla notices excitement in the man's voice, mustered with pride. "We couldn't hope for more in the short term. True, the houses are creaky, and the walls are hardly there.

Even the bridges struggle to stand. Yet, I think we can make it work."

A rider comes and whispers into Rasterforn's ear. The two exchange quick words before the other runs to relay orders.

"We are still looking for a safe place to put the kids," Rasterforn explains.

"Kids? Do you have children?" Nialla asks.

Rasterforn returns with a bewildering gaze. "Not me. No. But I have families in my charge. Infants."

"And it's difficult to have a nursery when everything's falling apart," Sackery understands. He sets aside his sword and saunters to Nialla, resting his hands on her shoulders. "We know that struggle all too well. Rushing from one place to the next, never staying anywhere for long? Not ideal for the young ones."

"Since we came into the valley, the children have had trouble sleeping," Rasterforn tells them.

"Almost like they're drowning on dry land?" Nialla asks.

Rasterforn raises his chin, studying her from the door. "Yes? Quite insightful for a five-summer child," he attests, confusion overtaking his friendly tone. "What are you people doing this far south? After the things I've seen along the way, the wilds are no place for children."

"We can handle ourselves," Sackery voices, stepping in to stare Rasterforn down.

"I didn't mean to insinuate, Master Greywolfe," the man quickly raises his hands and surrenders. "It's only that none of you look like simple travelers. Your clothes are too rich, though worn over time, by all appearance. And there's only two . . . three . . . four of you? Are you Aenümorian? No. Lúcran's folk wander in set patterns, following the seasons. And you? Maralfram—?"

"Miralifrim," Sackery corrects.

"What?"

"It's pronounced . . . Mira . . . lif . . . rim," Sackery utters slowly.

"Miralifrim," Rasterforn repeats. "As I was saying—?"

"You've said enough," Sackery stops him, although calm in his aggression.

Nialla flinches. It would seem like a casual statement to an ordinary man, but to Rasterforn, it is a noticeable threat. Nialla watches the commander take a few steps back, swallowing hard, sensing a line in the sand.

Grasping the moment, Nialla jumps forward and tugs on Rasterforn's arm. "Please stay with us awhile," she invites.

Sackery relaxes his posture as Nialla brings the man to their fire.

"That's very kind of you, little one," Rasterforn smiles.

"You welcomed us," Nialla says. "Now, let us welcome you."

She catches the glint of her mother's eye as they go to sit down, pretending to be asleep.

Sackery hangs by the door for a moment, deciding. He eventually nods and joins them at the fire. "We've seen our share of betrayals," the Vedrethal admits to the commander.

"Caution is never a bad thing. For what my word is worth, thank you for your patience."

Nialla's mother and Yeavengeritt stir awake now they've company to entertain.

"Don't lose sleep on my account," Rasterforn returns. "Everything's out of balance. All we can do is keep our heads above the water."

"You've no idea," her mother murmurs.

"Nobody likes change," Sackery admits. "But that's life. It's cruel, but what isn't? We can follow the course of a river to its end or drown fighting it."

"Except not everybody knows how to swim," Nialla shudders, tucking her knees into her chest.

"But not every river is rough, little one," Rasterforn frowns. "Lords and kings always want to row upstream."

"Holding onto the past, forgetting there's a future," Cyridel recites.

"Sometimes a people want to rise above lordly flags and banners," Rasterforn sighs.

"Declaring themselves kings by a self-defined right?" Sackery charges.

Rasterforn holds his stare for a moment. "Is that better or worse?" he asks.

People call to each other outside the door, and Nialla listens. Lord Rasterforn leans forward, but he's relaxed and unconcerned. He's used to the bustle of coming to a new place, setting up camp, tending to the horses and beasts of burden. Nialla hears the low rumble of wagons skidding on the cobblestones, soldiers marching as they pass the door to patrol the ruined streets.

"May I ask you a question, Lord Commander?" Nialla asks the man.

Rasterforn meekly frowns. "I am not a true lord," he says. "I bleed red, not blue. But go ahead."

"About what you said. That people want to rise above flags and banners," Nialla repeats. "What do you mean?"

The man drops his shoulders and turns to the fire between them. "Why does anybody resent generals and kings? Now, I have nothing against Nasuria Endúcar. She's Queen of Greater Maheira, with Calidor at its heart. But she's not her forebearers. Her brothers—*Taherian* and *Fredrelian*—were soldiers, and they died fighting."

Nialla shifts uneasily at the mention of her father's name. Her mother often refers to him as *Galron*, which he only took *after* they met.

"And she's not like them?" Nialla asks.

"No. She's a regalian," Rasterforn chides. "A politician."

"We hear that Queen Nasuria constantly battles with her court," Sackery probes for rumors.

"Talks of governance beyond my station," Rasterforn chides. "Even in the army, I hadn't the interest."

"And what about Lord Caedairen? Or the others in residence at the High Tower?"

"The Messenger? I never met him," Rasterforn admits. "But

I do know the Vedrethal well enough. I worked alongside them on occasion. They're decent folk, always lending a hand to people when they need it. Mostly. But I know soldiers, and despite their roles as peacekeepers who serve the crown, the Vedrethal tend to have an overly strict sense of duty. *Killers*."

"Is that how everyone sees them now?" Sackery frowns.

"Maybe the oldest among them used to be scholars?" Rasterforn answers.

"And the youngest?"

"Those I knew were orphans that spent decades training to fight," the man offers.

Nialla watches as Sackery feels his neck, letting out an unsteady sigh.

Rasterforn looks at him with consideration.

"Warrior-servants," Nialla describes.

Yeavengeritt stirs, listening quietly in the corner.

Rasterforn presses his palms together and looks at Nialla's mother with a soft sense. "Who *are* all of you?" he asks.

"We've told you our names," Cyridel offers.

"For some reason, I have this feeling you haven't."

A feeling? Nialla squints at him, having a feeling of her own like water poured over her head. This *man*, this "Lord Commander" to these strangers in a strange land . . . He's not merely another soldier putting an old life behind him. No. He called *Lúcran* by name. A name her mother told stories about when it came to the Aens.

Lúcran is the Herreavossall of the *Aen'klanen*. He is the

leader of all the Aenümorian clans.

Nialla crawls to him, reaching for his hand. "May I see?" she asks.

Rasterforn draws back, swallowing when he notices her eyes.

He gives her his arm. Nialla, in turn, removes the glove and finds the mark that denotes a proud heritage.

"You are Aenürial," Cyridel speaks it first, sitting taller. Her expression quickly shifts to a smile. "Lúcran's folk. Descendants of—?"

Rasterforn shakes his head. "I know *what* I am. Mixed blood, they called me."

"Mixed?" Sackery repeats, rubbing the back of his hand.

Commander Rasterforn bites his lips as if he's ashamed. "My father was of the Credamar," he admits. "But I grew up in Calidor with my mother and her family. The others? I am 'Lord Commander' because *she* was of a higher station, but I was a bastard. Acknowledged by my family but unwelcomed by my grandparents." His eyes fall on Sackery again.

"And you never thought to look for your father's *klanen*?"

"Where should I start? I have responsibilities," Rasterforn mourns, pulling his hand away. "And the Aens like to stay on the move."

Nialla blinks after realizing she's allowed her curiosity to get the better of her. She falls back next to the fire and stares into the flames. Ever slightly, the light grows, filling more of the room.

"My mother's mother was of the Verrol," Cyridel tells the man. "And my mother? She spent her early years with her clan until meeting my father during the Battle of the White Hills. He was a Míran Lord who fought in support of Anmoric after the Hadorns attacked the encampment at the Medhan Fuer."

Rasterforn smiles. "I figured you weren't exactly human," he nods.

"We're all human," Sackery corrects him. "It's only that some of us look different."

"And what are you, Greywolfe?" Rasterforn asks before dropping his eyes to Nialla. "What is she?"

"I thought you didn't care about our business?" Sackery argues.

"Your reason for being here, I couldn't care less," Rasterforn acknowledges. "But *who* you are?"

"He told us his story," Nialla agrees. "He trusted *us* to know it. Shouldn't that mean we trust *him* with ours?"

Her mother's eyes flash fearfully to Sackery.

"Your daughter is wise beyond her years," Rasterforn frowns. "But if you are of both Aenürial and Ellúndar stock, then I can only guess she's much older than she appears." He sits up and leans toward Nialla, studying her in the light. "Six or seven . . . But your eyes? Your eyes." He closes his mouth and drops his shoulders.

Sackery stands and marches to the doorway.

"Thank you for your visit, Lord Rasterforn," the Vedrethal says. "Please leave us be."

"I didn't mean to intrude," Rasterforn says with a crack in his tone.

"We know you didn't," Sackery accepts.

"Give us some time to talk about it," Cyridel urges. "It'll be for the best."

"I understand," Rasterforn breathes.

"You have your people to look out for," Sackery decides. "And we have ours."

"We all left our old lives behind," Rasterforn explains. "You, like us, probably want to forget."

"Not always," Nialla issues. She catches a tightness in the man's throat. Rasterforn knows there's more to this than simple travelers on the road, but Nialla can't guess how much he's figured out. "We have our secrets, Commander. Just like you have yours."

Rasterforn rises and dusts off his trousers. "Then I can only hope your secrets don't put my people at risk," he says.

Yeavengeritt coughs and spits. So much that it startles Rasterforn.

"Your people staying in this place puts them at risk," the Maithandír warns.

"Is that a threat, old man?" Rasterforn demands.

"A truth," Yeavengeritt spouts.

"Please," Cyridel urges.

"I will look for you and explain," Sackery promises. "But we would like to be alone for now."

Rasterforn eyes Yeavengeritt with suspicion before spinning on his heel. "I will hold you to that, Master Greywolfe. When you're ready, we can talk."

"By that time," Yeavengeritt adds, "it'll be too late for us."

"Too late? What do you mean?" Rasterforn asks.

"There's a danger to this place," Nialla tells him. "You felt it. As do we. Be on the lookout for Crows."

"And what do *birds* have to do with it?"

Nialla's mother shifts uneasily. "We don't know. I don't think we're dealing with mere birds."

"We found depictions of a three-headed crow," Sackery warns. "Something to do with what happened to this city?"

"I saw it, too. Three heads, six wings? A sigil?" Rasterforn begs the question.

"It's hard to say," Cyridel admits.

"And I don't think we want to be surprised when it makes its presence known," Sackery finishes.

Rasterforn blinks at them before letting out a breath. "I'll tighten my patrols until we can figure it out. If there's a danger on the loose, we'll catch it on the back foot."

"But they already know," Yeavengeritt stammers, sinking into his blankets. "You saw the bodies! The battle? All we can do is hide."

Rasterforn straightens his stance. "Great uncle, huh?" he asks.

"A survivor," Sackery seethes. "Now, would you please?" He motions to the door.

"Ask for me when you decide you are ready," Rasterforn

says, walking out of the building.

Nialla can feel a cold heat coming off him. It lingers for several minutes after he leaves. The room goes silent, her mother sensing it, the same as her.

Sackery paces along the wall by the door, his boots collecting dust as he moves. "Do you still trust him?" he asks.

"He's more astute than most we come across," Cyridel admits. "We can't lie to him. He's like us."

"He can feel it," Nialla whispers.

Sackery opens his mouth, stops, and closes it again.

"And so can they," Yeavengeritt coughs.

"Your Crows?" Sackery demands.

"First, the birds will come," the Maithandír describes. "Then the ground will beat like a drum. Footfalls. Each a wound, causing the earth to crack like ice under some heavy thing. I know their signs. And when to hide. For the rest of you? Maybe I can help? But maybe I can't, and they'll *take* you like they *took* the rest. Abominations."

Nialla glances at Yeavengeritt. Even now, he's in so much pain that it radiates off him, much like Rasterforn, only worse.

She was inside his mind for moments, piecing together fragments of his self-image, like repairing broken pottery or shattered glass. Nialla only numbed the pain, allowing a few small traces to break through the fog. But she found one place that felt more alive than anywhere else. Somebody had bottled all his good memories and hid them, burning her when she tried to take a peek.

"All we can do is wait and see what happens," Nialla says.

"You will lose," Yeavengeritt warns.

"No. We'll get through it," Sackery refuses. "All of us."

"You have us now," Nialla promises, squeezing Yeavengeritt's arm and comforting him.

Yeavengeritt returns with an awkward smile. He covers her hand with his own, so thin and weak.

"Thank you, my dear," he weeps. "Let us hope you are right."

— 9 —

IN PLAIN SIGHT

They find the baths while exploring the castle on the cliffs.

Nialla runs her hand through the water. "Warm?" she asks, looking up at Cyridel with those large, silver eyes.

Cyridel walks to the pool's edge, feeling the heat come off the water. "Hot springs," she describes. "But this far into the forest? These cliffs must have resulted from earthquakes years before they built the city. The ancient Maithandír likely saw it as a good, defensible position."

"How do you know that?" Nialla asks her.

"I don't, but it's a lovely story," Cyridel admits. "Baths like these were for lovers, not to wash."

"But it's all right if we do?" the girl asks.

"Nobody's been here for a long time," Cyridel decides, looking at the dust on the reliefs carved into the walls. "How long since your last bath?"

"I don't remember," Nialla smirks.

"Then what are you waiting for? Jump in," she instructs.

Nialla removes her boots, unbuttoning her shirt before plunging into the water. Cyridel does the same, but not before folding their clothes and putting them aside. Walking into the pool, she outstretches her arms, feeling the heat, letting it steal her breath.

"Does this place remind you of home?" Nialla asks.

"A little," Cyridel admits. "Ilhivendal was more spread across the mountain slopes. Most of the buildings were open, with floors built into the rock. Something my father learned from the hadorns, and it proved useful in warding off the cold winters. Trebunor? It's more . . . enclosed, like an enclave sitting at the edge of civilization. The façade of a kingdom, the depth of an outpost."

She pulls her daughter close and runs her fingers through Nialla's braids.

Nialla floats there, allowing the little ripples of their movement to create waves that bounce off the bath's ceramic tiles.

"That sounds nice," the girl whispers.

"It was," Cyridel smiles, realizing it slowly becomes a frown.

Nialla looks at her with those silver eyes, the water ringing her face. "You're sad?" she asks.

"I am never sad around you," Cyridel admits. "But I won't lie. I miss the days I could walk the cherry trees while they blossom in the young spring." She puts a hand to her heart and closes her eyes. "Or the view of the city on the bridge during misty days, the sunlight gleaming through from behind the mountains. Bright hues, overgrown pathways, and a tree in every house."

"Overgrown?"

Cyridel downturns her eyes to the girl and surrenders a genuine smirk. "Vines from the lower reaches would entangle with the flowers on the walkways," she describes. "They formed a beautiful interweave, reflecting the whites and blues that enamored the whole of Ilhivendal."

Nialla lifts a foot and dunks under the water.

As the girl breaks the surface, Cyridel snatches her, pulling her close.

Nialla squeals like a rabbit caught in a trap.

"Let me go!" Nialla giggles. But no matter how much the girl squirms, Cyridel hugs her tighter.

"I will never let you go," Cyridel laughs.

Footsteps echo from the corridor leading into the room. In these ruined halls, every sound erupts like thunder. Cyridel releases Nialla and swims to the pool's lip to see the silhouettes of three people—two women with a small girl between them, the latter about the same common age as Nialla.

But it's not until the three get closer that they see Nialla and Cyridel naked in the water.

"Oh! We're so sorry," the eldest of the women speaks.

The second woman, a bit younger, stares intently at Cyridel. "You're a—?" she begins, quickly stopping her thought.

"We didn't know anybody would be down here," the first

woman says.

"That's quite all right," Cyridel nods, sinking into the water.

"We heard laughter," the second woman explains. "We didn't mean to intrude. But? This place is so big! It's easy to get lost."

Cyridel offers them a kind nod. "You're only lost if you can't find your destination," she comforts.

"And if you don't have a destination," Nialla states, "can you be lost?"

Cyridel arches her arm and splashes the girl with a big wave.

"The water looks warm," the other little girl says.

"From hot springs that nestle under the city," Nialla tells her.

Cyridel catches a glint in her daughter's eye, staring at the other girl with . . . surprise, maybe glee?

The other shows off a big smile. Perfect teeth. An inviting face if ever there was one.

"You're welcome to stay if you want," Cyridel offers. "Plenty of room for everybody." She swims over to the edge and climbs out of the water, making her way to her clothes. Nialla is more hesitant for *obvious* reasons. "We were about to leave, ourselves. It's been ages since we last had a warm bath."

Cyridel catches the two other women staring at her as she dresses. Their faces are red, embarrassed. Yet, they don't look away.

"We're all women," Cyridel justifies. "Nothing to hide."

"It's improper," the eldest woman shudders.

"I grew up in a place where we celebrated the natural body," Cyridel explains. "And all its flaws."

"You have no flaws," the second woman laughs, clearly more at ease.

Cyridel holds a stare for a moment longer before glancing at the younger girl between them. "And why are you here?" she works the courage to ask.

"What . . . What do you mean?" the first returns.

Cyridel helps Nialla out of the water and throws a cloak over her shoulders. "It doesn't matter," she admits, turning to the women starkly. Only for the strangest thing to happen . . . The other girl jumps forward, like she's playing a game of rabbits, and extends a hand to her daughter.

"I am Ankara," she says.

"Nialla," her daughter says, looking down at it, confused.

"Hi, Nialla."

"Beautiful name," Cyridel steers.

"Her father always had a way with words," the second woman softly smiles. "I am Mrillane, Ankara's mother. And this is my sister, Desre. She's not very trusting until you get her talking. Then, you can't get her to stop."

"That's not true," Desre shushes.

"Oh, it's quite true," Mrillane laughs.

"And what's your name, dearie?" Desre asks, looking at Cyridel.

Cyridel doesn't answer, not at first. She stands there awkwardly, like a deer stuck in the lamplight.

"My name?" she asks, having to think about it.

"Yes? Your name," Desre reassures. "It's all right."

"Miralifrim," Cyridel fights to say. "That's what they call me. Miralifrim."

"A striking name for a striking woman," Mrillane follows. "I've never seen anybody like you. Your ears? Pretty things."

"There's some Ellúndar blood in me," Cyridel admits.

"More than *some*, don't you think?" Desre weighs.

Cyridel nods, but her willingness to continue falls short. "We should head back," she tells Nialla.

"Already?" the girl returns.

"You don't have to go," Mrillane suggests. "Maybe we can talk more?"

"Talk? Aren't you three exploring this place?" Cyridel asks, feeling a tinge numbing her throat.

"And why shouldn't we?" Desre demands. "Ankara was born on the road. We made do with what we had."

"With it always seeming like there's never enough," Cyridel whispers.

"Yes," Desre praises with a satisfied grin.

"This place is so beautiful," Mrillane says cheerfully. "But it's so broken, decayed. What happened here? A storm? Plague?"

"We don't know," Cyridel admits.

"You are from the group Lord Rasterforn found when we arrived?" Desre asks.

"You heard about that?"

"Word travels fast among the caravan," Mrillane explains. "That, and we've never met you."

"Perhaps you *did* and merely forgot?" Cyridel suggests.

"We'd remember your face, Lady Miralifrim," Desre denies. "But details get muddy after one too many lips."

Cyridel softens her stance, threading Nialla's braids behind her head. It still doesn't feel right. She is lying to these people, even after all these years. Her name isn't Miralifrim; it is what strangers know her by these days. It's the name of Eéwen's mother, a friend since childhood. Nobody outside Ilhivendal would've heard it.

But that doesn't stop a twisting inside her chest, causing her heart to sink into her stomach.

"Are there others with you?" Cyridel asks.

"Many," Mrillane answers. "People from all over."

"That's not wholly what I—" she pauses, but only momentarily. "It doesn't matter."

"No, no," Desre utters. "Speak your mind."

"We should go," Cyridel says, apprehensive, taking Nialla by the arm.

"The only way through the hard days is by staying together," little Ankara says. "Always together."

Nialla pulls her arm away and frowns. "*Vi kan vaere sammen*," she offers. "Always."

The two girls draw close, touching hands. Cyridel watches as the air between them brightens, like the sun through cracks in the clouds. After so many decades on the road, Nialla rarely had a chance to make friends. But as she witnesses it now? Cyridel is a little heartbroken, knowing how it will likely end.

She wipes a tear rolling down her cheek.

Looking at the newcomers, they seem happy, almost as if they're glad they aren't the only ones left to wander.

Her lip trembles, terrified.

Does she have the strength to let them in? Time kills the strongest men—the only enemy an army can't defeat, no matter how large or well-trained. Much as time eroded Trebunor, the two girls, Ankara and Nialla, speak as if all they can see is each other.

"A little hope," Cyridel mutters.

But the stonework shifts and groans as she says it . . . hope, with a cold breeze pushing the dust in from the corridor.

"What is that noise?" Desre begs the question.

"Maybe this isn't the safest place to talk," Cyridel suggests. 'This city's old. Unkempt."

"She's right," Mrillane agrees. "This whole place could fall on our heads."

"Are you three set for tonight? Do you know where you'll be staying?"

"With everybody else," Desre answers. "The soldiers found a tower overlooking the lower courtyard."

"You're welcome to join us if you'd like," Mrillane suggests. "Do you have any stories from your travels? Ankara loves to hear stories! We raised her on legends over the years, so it'll be nice to tell her something else for a change." She offers

Cyridel her arm.

Cyridel bites down on her molars. "And what tales does Ankara like?" she asks, looping elbows with the woman.

Ankara looks at her after giggling with Nialla.

"How about a love story?" the girl asks.

"Maybe the one about the Old King and the Mountain Princess?" Mrillane suggests.

"She's heard that one before," Desre tells her sister.

"It's her favorite," Mrillane returns, turning to Cyridel. "Do you know it, Miralifrim?"

"A version of it," she frowns, tightening the belt around her waist. "What is it called again?"

"Galron and Cyridel," Desre describes. "Another fable, if you ask me."

"They say it's a true story," Mrillane corrects.

"Hogwash the *elves* tell to make themselves seem better than us," Desre argues. "No offense." She glances at Cyridel, then at Mrillane.

"I don't believe that."

"Then you are a fool, sister."

"Not a fool," Cyridel says, raising her chin. "A dreamer. Somebody who believes."

"And what does she believe?"

"In fairytales," Nialla speaks, punctuated with a smile.

– Trebunor's ruined halls –

— 10 —

LONGER JOURNEY'S PAST

Sackery walks the battlements above the streets of this decrepit city. Two bridges accent the two gates that pass through the walls—the first over the west river fork, the artisan bridge that led to Trebunor's trade district, and the smaller forest bridge, where most travelers on the eastern road would arrive.

The last time he stood on these stones, before recent events, it wasn't a city but a town with a fortress on the cliffs overlooking the fertile valley.

He remembers an outpost at Mireaderal to the southeast, garrisoned by a calvary unit, hundreds strong. Sackery reckons that many of the Maithandír they found on the battlefield north of the river were the remains of that unit. They mustered their forces and answered a threat, only to die in the dirt.

Sackery likely knew some of those faces in the mud. They

helped him hunt for the Doomed King at the end of Icurian's War.

Wayndrin of Nurindeon . . . Felandor of the White . . . Caeldrin Halfheart . . .

"Heroes, carried by the winds," Sackery murmurs. "Born as legends."

He watches the woods on the other side of Trebunor's wall, waiting for a sign.

Throughout the city, there are more depictions of crows . . . Some are familiar, like the crows with three heads and six wings. Other times, he saw images of a snake with the head and wings of a bird, feathers as black as charcoal, sometimes drawn with a white outline.

But what does it mean? He doesn't know a monster of the like.

Ambient spirits stalk the wildwoods, taking many forms. Much like snakes, but not with bird-like features.

Not only that, but the symbols form a circle, with the heads devouring the tails of whichever body it possesses—snake or crow, it doesn't matter.

"Am I interrupting?" a voice jumps out from behind him.

Sackery turns to find Rasterforn there with his Captain-of-the-Watch.

"Just keeping an eye on the woods," Sackery admits.

"Afraid that some shadow-beast is going to prowl out of the dark and haunt the streets?" the Captain mocks.

Lord Rasterforn raises a hand to steady his second-in-command.

"Happened before in these parts," Sackery tells him.

"Before?" Rasterforn asks.

Sackery clenches his jaw. "A turn of phrase," he corrects.

"And I thought the lies were behind us," Rasterforn frowns.

"What do you want me to say?" Sackery asks. "The people who built this city had an army to defend themselves. So, if they abandoned this place, it wasn't done lightly."

Surprise flickers on the man's face, almost as if he didn't expect Sackery's next words to make sense. He nods to the Captain, who leaves and heads toward the courtyard. He has a job, and it's not to talk to Sackery about bumps in the night.

"And these Crows the old man went on about?" Rasterforn weighs. "How can *birds* do all this?"

"Unless they're not birds," Sackery suggests.

"A name, then?"

"Something akin to a moniker. Yes."

"Master Greywolfe? Tell me. Please?"

"An army? A natural disaster?"

"These streets were worn down by time," Rasterforn points out. "Not razed."

"And speculation will only cause us to prepare for the wrong foe," Sackery warns.

Rasterforn surrenders a grim smile before pivoting toward the courtyard with the dead weodemair tree. Below them, the man's people are busy putting the final touches on their camp. Soldiers patrol the streets with sentries on the walls, watching the Seclumor Wilds. The air steadily darkens as the evening becomes night.

"You're an odd one, Master Greywolfe," Rasterforn chuckles, studying him carefully. "Answer me truthfully for a change. Where *are* you from? Your accent?"

"A little ways north," Sackery describes. "And a long way west."

"A long way? How long?"

Sackery looks the man in the eye for a moment. "A very long way," he answers.

Rasterforn grumbles under his breath before squaring his shoulders. "Then, let me guess," he asks politely.

"At your will," Sackery nods.

The man circles him, looking Sackery from head to boot. He reaches and feels the threads of his cloak, tapping the bracers of his gloves and eyeing the engravings on the crossguard of his sword. "The quality of your arms is more than what a poor man could buy," Rasterforn states. "Your clothes are old but finely sewn. Worn down, like this place. And what do they hide?" He hesitates before lifting Sackery's coat to see the armor underneath. "That's a story you carry with you, Master Greywolfe. Isn't it?"

Sackery's expression remains passive, unwilling to answer. "Must I say it?" he asks.

Rasterforn shrugs and walks to the wall's edge. "Vedrethal," he finally says.

The word ringing from his tongue sends a shiver through

the air that causes the trees outside the city to shift and bellow.

"You are a clever man, Lord Rasterforn," Sackery confirms.

"Not clever. At least, I don't pretend to be," Rasterforn exhales. "I—? I tend to notice things."

"And what about you? You said a few hundred followed you," Sackery adds. "But down there? That's more than a few."

"Did you do a counting?"

"As much as I was able to."

"So, it seems we're both liars."

"How many?"

"Five thousand?"

"Five—? You don't sound too sure."

"It changes as we go. With only seven hundred fighters to protect them," Rasterforn admits. "Not enough."

"Why didn't you tell me?"

"For the same reason you kept your *real* self a secret," the man laughs.

"I have my wards to protect," Sackery argues.

"And I have *these* people," Rasterforn iterates. "For better or worse, they're with me."

Sackery watches as the man presses his palm to his breastplate. It weighs on the commander, their lives . . . Much as Cyridel and Nialla rely on the Vedrethal. Years ago, Sackery swore to Taherian Endúcar to keep his family hidden, to keep them safe. And he's done the best he could against many dangers.

But they are no longer facing brigands and highwaymen. No. The chill in the air shifts wildly the more he pays attention to it, almost like it's getting a measure of him, figuring out how he'd react. Sackery only knows a few beings capable of such feats, and none are good omens.

Colorful sparks fly across the courtyard. Groups dance in the streets, with hundreds more singing unabashedly. Joyful, even.

"Fireworks?" Sackery asks.

"A celebration."

"For what?"

"Life? People don't always need a reason."

"It's dangerous without knowing what's out there."

"As well pushing folk beyond their limits," Rasterforn warns, stepping forward. "Sometimes? They need to let loose."

Sackery goes to lean against the wall's inner crenel, watching the festivities—new life in a dead place. Shadows pass in front of the bonfires, lighting the faces of the dancers. Even from this distance, they seem to glow with reverence, like the face of a mother holding their newborn child for the first time.

And in that moment, the air gets cold when a small bird lands next to him, black and beady.

Is it a raven? No. It's a crow.

That's when he notices more of them on the rooftops. Dozens. Hundreds? All looking down at the newcomers, the people celebrating a chance at finding a new home. And among the murderous flocks, one bird sits white against the black, violet eyes beaming at him, and *only* him. Warm, not cold.

Sackery's mouth agapes, and he draws back.

"Shanashéron?"

— 11 —

WHISPERS IN THE NIGHT

She touches her mother's arm to see if she's awake.

Ankara waddles next to her, huddled under a blanket. "Is she asleep?" she asks her.

Nialla holds her breath as her mama stirs quietly. "I think so?"

"Then you can show me your trick?"

"I don't want people to see us."

"How about down by the tree? I saw a flowerbed," Ankara urges.

"That's in the middle of the camp," Nialla frowns.

"And who'd pay attention to a couple of girls sitting by the fireside?" Ankara smirks. "Trust me."

Nialla looks into the girl's blue eyes, her dark blonde hair dressed in braids, much like hers. But then she looks around at the people in the tower—most of them asleep. One or two soldiers patrol the rows, keeping an eye on the windows and the doors, watching the few still awake playing dice in the corner.

This caravan journeyed from place to place these last several years, never staying anywhere too long.

Nialla feels a twist in her throat, understanding what that does to a person.

She grew up eating what they could on the trailside—small berries, wild game—food that's difficult to digest. It's not the comfort her mother knew in Ilhivendal. Yet, it's all *she* has ever known.

"Okay," Nialla agrees. "Down the stairs, across the courtyard."

"And by the tree," Ankara smiles.

"Just one trick," Nialla returns the gesture. "A small one."

Ankara picks herself off the floor and hurries to the stairwell. The tower to the courtyard is a busier path, with soldiers and settlers all finding spaces to stay before it gets too dark. Outside, riders lead their horses to makeshift stables in the larger buildings. Wagons and beasts of burden shuffle through the wide alleyways, marchers signaling to the waggoneers when to stop.

The girls dodge the amblers. Nialla falls behind Ankara, who is more used to the bustle of camp life's early stages.

Every once in a while, Sackery would bring them to a larger town for supplies. Nialla had never seen so many people in one place, almost stepping over each other, at times, making her feel small, like a face in the masses. And now, what's worse, she can hear them, their raw emotions.

Stark rivalries . . . Genuine friendships . . . Bitter hatreds . . . Fleeting affections . . .

Nialla's chest throbs as she finds it harder to breathe.

She stops as they fall under the burnt weodemair's branches, the shadow of its ashen trunk enclosing around her.

Ankara walks up next to her, taking her hand. "Are you okay?" she asks.

"I don't—? I don't know," Nialla fights to say the words.

She stumbles to the rocks that circle the tree, suddenly breathing too much. Closing her eyes, Nialla focuses on her heartbeat, the wind's subtle sway as it caresses the banners and flags the caravan has draped around the courtyard. She listens to the fireworks, the singing in the distance, the crackling of the bonfires.

Ankara joins her, wrapping her arms around Nialla's shoulders. "Nells? You look sick," she murmurs.

"I am drowning," Nialla shudders, crossing her arms, suddenly cold.

But she doesn't feel cold. Not ever.

Nialla leans back and listens to the old men singing their high songs and younger women dancing to the words, slow and steady.

And for a moment, the darkness burns away:

'Neath the cliffs at the First King's strait,

Three daughters stand at the beach's gate,
O'mair, o'mair,
The three girls shout,
'Twas a bittersweet tune,
There on the shore of their first love's flame,
Joy steals the younger's shame,
And they shan't forget the dance they've had,
Along the spirited tides,
Sweeping left, stepping right,
Swinging high in the bright moonlight,
The sands are bare as the waves roll where to,
They bury their childhood pride.

"Strange words," Nialla suggests.

"They sing about the children of the First King," Ankara describes. "Aamelian had four heirs—three daughters and a son. Tealian was the oldest and would become King of Calidor after Aamelian died on the shores, fighting a sea-beast that threatened to pull the city down from the cliffs."

"But why were his daughters on the beach?" Nialla asks.

"Some people think the song is about the youngest daughter finding love where her father died."

"And it's not?"

"Not the way my mother tells it," Ankara frowns.

"Then how does she tell it?" Nialla asks.

"That the first love's flame is about the love a father has for his children."

"They went there to mourn him?"

"To remember what they lost," Ankara tells her. "At least, that's how I always heard it."

Nialla surrenders a subtle grimace. "They wanted to bury that loss," she whispers, "so they could move on with their lives." A tale that makes her heart weep, like the leaves in Autumn about to fall. She knows those names . . . *Aamelian, Tealian* . . . her father's fathers, the old kings of men. "Vedreron."

She turns to the burnt weodemair tree, its branches long since dead. Nialla can tell it was once a proud thing, standing tall in the thoroughfare, a victim of whatever happened to this city that drove its people out. She presses her forehead bare against the bark, closing her eyes to listen.

There's a quietness to it, like a steady beating of a drum or a heart, thudding through its skin and into her.

It's breathing . . . strained, but it's there. Alive? Somehow. But in so much pain, Nialla pulls away.

Around her, all the noise quiets down. Ankara looks at her, lips moving, but only a squeaky voice comes out of them. Fireworks rocket overhead, but all she hears is the sudden pop when they explode. Children scream as they run from their parents. Are they chasing each other? She allows the music to rush through her in waves, feeling the strings hum while the people step to the rhythm.

Nialla drops back, letting out a clean breath.

"What was that?" Ankara asks, her words finally heard.

"Lost myself for a moment," Nialla cries. "I had to find an

anchor."

"Is that normal?"

"For me? When it comes, it's hard to control."

She looks upward at the tree and its branches again. Under, there's a bed of flowers, withered and dry.

They died long ago, but the earth decided to leave them. Nialla frowns, her hands cold. Dead things don't stay untouched by the natural order. All life fades into the dirt, returning the energy to the cycle, the progression of death and rebirth.

Nialla leans forward and scoops one of the flowers with her hands.

Ankara watches. "Is this your trick?" she asks.

Nialla glances at her before offering the girl a smile.

She brings the flower to her mouth: "*Allanen vahru*," Nialla whispers. "*Belloquarth sorndenen*." All the fires in the courtyard burn a little brighter as she speaks. And as the air warms, the flower petals glow white, breathing new life.

Ankara sits next to her, pupils enlarged, reflecting the firelight. "How did you do that?" she wonders.

"I sing to it," Nialla smiles. "A little whisper to remind it of what it lost." She puts the flower back where it belongs, padding the soil and watching it feed the others in the bed. "The old allowed to breathe again."

The girls stare at the petals as they radiate from white to yellow. All the colors? Vibrant again.

Rebirth and return.

Above them, on the rooftops of the courtyard, black eyes

watch them. Crows, hundreds of them, fill the spaces between the light. And one mingling in the middle of them, white as snow with spots on its wings. Nialla can't keep her eyes away as it swoops to a perch. With violet eyes, almost purple, glowing against the night.

But it's not looking at her. No. Outward, toward Trebunor's walls.

"Sackery?"

A scream cracks the air!

Everything goes silent far too quickly.

The noise stops the dancers. Everyone in the courtyard falls back, soldiers drawing their spears and shields.

Nialla looks to find the white bird scared off, breaking hard against the wind.

Another blood-curdling shriek follows . . . and another . . . then a sixth . . . a tenth . . . It continues until what sounds like a dozen voices crying out at the end of their songs. Nialla feels them fading away like sand washing under a wave, drowning.

"Sackery!" Nialla calls out.

Like a cold dour flooding her mind, Nialla feels a spike pressed against her skull. She holds her breath, closing her fists, fighting it this time. It's as if something other is trying to force its way into her thoughts, to read her mind, her safe place—her fortress.

"Nells?" Ankara asks. "What's happening?"

Nialla throws off the pain and gets to her feet. Around her, the soldiers die in the shadows. All the bonfires go out, leaving them to battle alone, pulled into the dark. People clamor toward the weodemair tree. Their armor goes rent while their shields become splinters—blood on the ground, pooling in the gaps of the cobblestones.

They come from the forest, *the Crows*, like a tide through Trebunor.

She takes Ankara by the hand and runs to the tower. They'll be safe there, with her mother, where it's warm.

— 12 —

WHEN THE LIGHT DIES

Cyridel hears the scream and jumps from her covers. Nialla's not next to her.

Everybody in the tower now wakes up scared. The soldiers hurry to shuffle folks into the corner, away from the doors and window slits. Cyridel looks to the two women, Desre and Mrillane, in a near panic. Their daughter's missing, too . . . *Ankara? Did she leave with Nialla? Where did they go?*

Cyridel swallows, closing her eyes. She reaches for her pack and grabs her long knife, drawing it.

Her reflection stares at her through the metal.

Yeavengeritt catches her arm, his face twisted like he's looking at her through broken glass.

"They caught her song," he rambles. "Are they drawn to the source? Something familiar."

"What do you mean?" Cyridel asks.

"Remnants of Old Eedian," Yeavengeritt stammers. "Vedreron?"

A powerful chill hits the air, coming through the doors as he says it. Like it . . . knows the word. The fires in the tower's hearth fade like embers fighting a torrent.

Cyridel gets to her feet and pushes through the crowd, leaving the Maithandír behind. The soldiers by the door stand agitated, made clear by the smell of sweat dripping off them. Afraid. Even under their armor and pride, it's hard to hide.

"Return to the back, ma'am," one of them orders her.

"We must go help the people down there," Cyridel says calmly.

"Don't you hear that?" another chides.

"Screams . . . There's a fight," says a third. "People are dying."

"Our jobs are to stay here and protect these folk."

"And that's what we'll do."

Cyridel looks at the men with a sorrowful grace. Afraid, but not for herself. And *not* for themselves. She glances back at everybody in the room: sons standing with their fathers, daughters helping their mothers to keep a confused peace. Cyridel is only a stranger to them, so she doesn't matter. They look out for their own.

"I *am* leaving," Cyridel decides.

"And do what?" a soldier demands.

"To look for my daughter and her friend."

"You want to go out there? Don't you hear *that* noise?"

"I hear it," Cyridel nods. "And I feel it. Like men drowning on dry land."

"How do you—?"

"Just let her go!" another shouts.

"Close the door behind her!"

The soldier's eyes fall on her with water running down his cheeks.

"We won't help you if there's trouble," the man says.

"I wouldn't expect it," Cyridel frowns.

The soldiers move out of the doorway and let her pass. It's an arduous trek down the stairs, with people crowding to get up. Cyridel has a light step, moving around the chaos, the panic, and the desperate souls that don't understand what's happening outside.

Neither does she. But her daughter must be out there, and she intends to find the girl.

At the bottom, more people rush in for a haven. Among them is Nialla and her new friend, Ankara.

The two girls look exhausted, but it is Nialla who looks worse.

Cyridel hurries and pulls her daughter aside, but the girl writhes, almost like she doesn't recognize her mother's hand.

"Nialla!" Cyridel shouts. "It's me. Do you hear me?"

But the girl is strong and pushes Cyridel against the wall, a red hue in her silver eyes.

"Mama?" Nialla cries.

"Look at me!" Cyridel settles. "Look at me."

Her tone meanders between a stern whisper and a subtle

warmth. It's enough to pull the girl out of whatever mind space she was in, submerged between what's real and the nightmares she can see while she's awake. "Mom," Nialla recites, letting out a slow breath.

Cyridel presses her hand against her daughter's chest, feeling her heartbeat.

"You'll be all right," Cyridel whispers, drawing Nialla close and hugging her tight.

Beside them, the other girl, Ankara, looks at them, pale and weeping. Cyridel takes her cloak and wraps it around the poor thing.

"Thank you," Ankara says, looking so cold.

"Are you two hurt?" Cyridel asks.

"No," Nialla mutters. "Out there . . . Something? Killing people."

Cyridel's jaw clenches. More folks rush into the tower, squeezing through the door. But it's narrow, and they're desperate. Rasterforn's people. Settlers, all of them looking for a new home, but instead, all they've found is death. They were celebrating. Singing and dancing for the joy they sought at the journey's start.

She closes her fist and pushes past them. Nialla follows her. Ankara? She stays back with everyone else.

Outside, it's dark. Farther along the avenue, Cyridel marches. She steps into the courtyard, one of many. Soldiers move fast, their spears and shields, swords, and bows ready in their hands. Rasterforn rises into the space, Sackery behind him.

He faces the gruesome scene that's played out around the burned weodemair tree.

Sackery notices them and hurries, leveling with Nialla, and kisses her on the head.

"Yeavengeritt was right," Cyridel tells him. "The Crows?"

"They've come," Nialla confirms.

Sackery offers a grimace. He looks around at the bodies and the soldiers moving to secure the courtyard. Whatever did this, it's gone. Dead birds litter the stonework, mixed with the bodies of Rasterforn's settlers. Cyridel watches the Vedrethal breathe, a weakness in his stance.

"A monster did this," Sackery utters, hate in his eyes.

Across the way, Cyridel spots Lord Rasterforn kneeling over some of the bodies.

"What's happened?" the man cries. "Somebody? Tell me!"

Cyridel moves in his direction, but Sackery steps in her way. "What are you doing?" she asks him.

"He's in grief," Sackery returns. "Confused."

"As are we," Nialla says.

"We've got a live one over here!" somebody shouts.

Cyridel takes a breath, tears running down her cheeks when Rasterforn's eyes snap up at them, then at the shouter. He wants to yell, as anybody would, but he doesn't. These are the commander's friends, a family he made on this journey . . . People whose names he's known since departing with them from Calidor.

Rasterforn marches to a group now gathering around the

survivor. "Berran? How the—?" he asks.

Cyridel leans into Sackery. "Berran?"

"Captain-of-the-Watch," the Vedrethal returns. "He was ahead of us."

"And now?"

"I don't know."

The three slowly approach the gatherers. Sackery paces around the carnage, eyeing the devastation. Cyridel stays in the crowd, Nialla in her arms.

Rasterforn hunches over the man, whispering to him. "Take it easy, deep breaths. What happened? Who did this? What—?"

Berran's lips shudder as he fights for the words. There's an obvious pain in the act, bleeding heavily.

"How ba-b-bad . . . is it?" the man stutters, red flooding his mouth.

"It feels worse than it looks," Rasterforn says to him.

It's a lie. Cyridel knows it's a lie, as do both men. A lie meant to comfort, but the captain has a hole in his chest, like something tore at him, looking to get inside.

Sackery stops alongside the pair, taking the wounded man's hand. Carefully, he presses the other's palm enough to block the nerves and help alleviate his pain. Rasterforn notices, his eyes resting on the Vedrethal with some little hope.

"Greywolfe?" Rasterforn begs the question. "How—?"

"This man saw what killed these people," Sackery explains. "We need to know. Focus, now. There isn't much time."

The two men look at Berran, whose breath becomes steadier but critically shallow. Cyridel raises a hand to her mouth, the emotions running off these people like rain on a mountain.

Rasterforn's eyes narrow at the Vedrethal, Yet he nods. He understands. It won't be long before the soldier is unable to speak.

"It's all right, Berran. You're a good man," Rasterforn says. "Let it out. Tell us what you saw."

More gather to listen. The soldiers move to cordon the courtyard, but they can do nothing to keep them from seeing what's on the ground.

"A sh-shadow . . . from the w-w-woods . . . surpassed our pa-p-patrols and lo-l-lookouts," Berran describes, spitting blood. "We th-thought it was pre-p-predators at first, so I pulled our sentries inside the city to see if we c-c-couldn't draw them into the o-o-open."

Sackery remains silent. Cyridel steps cautiously forward. She listens, the weight of the man's words squeezing her throat. A tingling at the back of her neck causes her to flinch, like a bucket of water washing over her. Nialla does the same. She feels it, too? A presence watching them from the rooftops.

She looks up to find nothing there, not even the birds. All dead on the ground.

"What else?" Rasterforn urges.

"It emerged on t-two legs . . . long and slender," Berran continues. "And it sw-s-swamped the c-courtyard. But w-when I arrived? We thought it was a w-w-woman, but s-something was . . . wrong with her. Not a . . . not a beast. She w-was pale, like a co-c-corpse, fresh f-f-from the grave. T-t-tattered cloak."

"Did it speak? Say her name?" Sackery demands.

"All I s-saw were Crows after that," Berran cries. "Crows? So . . . so m-many. Didn't you s-see them? Everywhere! So, m-many . . . little eyes . . . dark eyes . . . dead eyes." He stammers into incoherent ramblings, not unlike Yeavengeritt when they found him in the far tower. Then, the man stops talking entirely. His light fades, and his arm drops to the cold, hard ground.

Rasterforn closes his eyes. He stands, cuffing his hands around his neck.

"Greywolfe?" he asks. "What did this?"

Sackery lowers his shoulders and frowns. "I don't know."

"Don't tell me you don't know," Rasterforn growls. "You asked if it spoke! What did you expect him to say?"

"You don't want my answer to that," Sackery refuses.

"A monster? A story meant to scare little kids?"

Sackery rises suddenly and unapologetically, a scowl on his face.

Cyridel moves between the two men, her arms out to keep them from drawing their blades on one another. "Enough!" she shouts.

"Or what?" Rasterforn demands. "Look around us! Tell me what you see?"

Cyridel's lip trembles as she backs away. She looks at the dead, the soldiers, the dancers that filled this courtyard, once alive but now slaughtered. The armor of the troops, broken and shattered, like a great force had cleaved a rock through them, wrecking all that stood in its way, like a bear on a rampage.

Sackery softens his stance. "Stories. You hear about them as children," he speaks. "A hunter in the woods? Crows? You never expect them to come alive. But the shadows live . . . a past made manifest, like a terror feeding on scraps. Some call it a scavenger. Me? A twisted distortion, no better than a beast."

"What do you mean?" Rasterforn asks.

More arrive in the courtyard. Folks cry loudly. News of the massacre spreads quickly through the camps and the people who thought they were safe in this dead-stone city. Wives call for their husbands, the menfolk to their women. Several kids ask if anybody's seen their parents. They only get silence for an answer before the adults can push them away from the scene. Children shouldn't see the worst that life has to throw at them. Cyridel understands.

But little did she know that she walked Nialla into such a nightmare.

Sackery doesn't answer. He feels his palms drenched in red, the others combing over the dead.

The soldiers carry the bodies, resting them in lines under the burned weodemair tree.

Rasterforn doesn't break his stare. "Greywolfe? You know what killed my people, don't you?"

Cyridel shifts her weight as Sackery looks at her, reluctant to turn in the good man's direction. "Do you know?" she asks.

"Greywolfe!" Rasterforn shouts, no longer calm. "What do you mean? What can do this? You're like a bird spotting its prey a league away."

Sackery remains tentative in his posture a moment longer before nodding his surrender. "Two? There are two beings I know that are capable of this," he describes. "The first? Those of Old Eedian—Vedrel—and their blood descendants, the Vedreron." He looks at Nialla next to Cyridel. "Neither have walked these lands since before Aamelian's landing at Nodrine. But the second? We call it a *gafling*, a monster of ancient times that feeds on the remnant power left behind by the former."

"Like parasites?" Rasterforn equates.

"Leeches. Dangerous when provoked," Sackery adds. "And it would explain a lot about this city."

Nialla moves away from Cyridel, joining Sackery at his side. "Monsters? Three of them?" she asks him, a crack in her voice.

"We can't give them a chance to attack again," Rasterforn decides, speaking with force. Loud enough to draw everyone's attention in the courtyard. Soldiers, mourners . . . They all look inward, at them, and at the tree, burned, but . . . not burnt, like the ash is washing away with the rest of the tide.

"But how do we do it? Tell me, Master Greywolfe. What do you suggest I do?"

Sackery stands there, his fingertips touching the pommel of his sword, Myheirad, its name. And when he draws it? There's always blood.

Cyridel knows it. As the world once did, long ago.

"You'd be a fool to fight it, Lord Rasterforn," Sackery warns him, urging the man's restraint.

"We can't let this go unpunished!"

"You can't punish this! Gaflings are vicious and cunning in their way," Sackery argues. "You kill them. But they are more than what your riders can handle. Not animals. *Monsters.* Evil from a time when the world was still dark. Untouched. But go ahead, track it down. What you'll find will turn your war party from hunters into prey. That, I promise you."

The courtyard goes silent at the brash warning. Every soul in earshot looks warily at one another—subtle glances, here and there, betraying their disbelief. After all, who *is* this outsider claiming to know this enemy that's attacked them? A stranger with an odd accent, flanked by a stranger woman and a child with silver eyes?

"He's right," Cyridel supports. "You can't fight it."

Sackery frowns at her, a look that cuts deeper than a blade.

"And who are *you* to say I can't?" Rasterforn barks his contempt.

"Because I've hunted gaflings before," Sackery claims, bowing his head in condolence. "Never alone, mind you.

My brothers and sisters always stood with me. The same story told a dozen ways. We made sure their endings were the same."

Rasterforn cocks his head in fascination.

"You say these gaflings are dangerous," he confides, lowering his gaze to young Nialla. "You say my soldiers cannot win against it. But now you're telling me that you've hunted and killed them before? How long since we met? A day? Maybe two? And you're demanding that I trust your word? Why? For what? Look at them! Forty men and women slaughtered by the claws of your monster."

"We are not talking about some rabid animal," Sackery says, raising his shoulders.

"But now you're telling me there's nothing I can do?"

Sackery maintains a serene expression as Rasterforn's tempter visibly grows.

Cyridel pushes to the edge, looking at the latter. He's more than Aenümorian, more than human . . . He almost feels . . . Ellúndar? Now, she understands that she's not the only one to lie. Rasterforn is a sad man, begging for more than a simple life.

"Kindred spirits," Cyridel whispers.

"And what does that mean?" Rasterforn asks.

Sackery smiles. "That we don't know each other," he finally breaks free. "And we never will, but I'm willing to fight."

"Fight a monster?"

"No. Kill it! Them? For you."

Rasterforn's demeanor changes as he spies the countenance among the crowd, recognizing the hope in their whispers. Sternness gives way to a content smile.

"The way you say that is eerily familiar, Master Greywolfe," Rasterforn asserts. "All right. What are you thinking?"

"Something that killed forty people won't be easy to beat," Cyridel frowns.

Sackery raises an eyebrow. "Just like that?" he questions.

"Would you offer to help us if you didn't mean it?" Rasterforn quandaries. "You travel with a woman and her daughter for no reason except a promise you made the father. You're not him. And if your looks are anything to go by—?" He glances at Nialla and Cyridel. "I won't stop you if you want to head off and die in the woods."

"He won't die," Nialla says, walking up to him.

"Is that so, little one?" Rasterforn smirks. "And why is that? All men die."

"Because he's the greatest swordsman in the world," Nailla claims.

"Can a man be so great? What does that mean except to say he's survived all his battles? Until now? Later? A century on? A thousand years, hence?" Rasterforn speaks with the grace of a man who thinks aloud. Cyridel knocks on his mind's walls, and he pushes back, aware of what she's trying to do. He looks at her. Frowns. Then tries to hide the frown with a mask. "Every soldier dies. No matter how strong he is, there's always someone . . . *something* . . . stronger than him."

"Don't worry," Sackery accepts. "I'll be fine."

Rasterforn bows his head. "I do hope you're right, Vedrethal. Dying in the woods? I don't want that to be your fate."

"Meanwhile, ready your people," Sackery orders. "Get them out of Trebunor."

"We intend to make this our home," Rasterforn refuses. "We'll dig in, hold our ground."

"And if I *do* fail?"

"Then we'll join the people who built this place."

"Another sour note in a dying song," Nialla attunes.

Rasterforn's face twists before turning to the gatherers. "Fianna? Get to work organizing the next watch!" he shouts orders. "Don't let them stand in the open this time! Airentám? Conrand? I want your men on alert! Let's find somewhere to put the dead where the carrion birds can't reach them."

Cyridel waits as the Maheirans get to work. Sackery is beside her, only stepping away when the courtyard empties.

She follows him to the old stables they stayed in during their first nights in Trebunor. He gathers a few trinkets he left there—a pack, cloak, and enough food to keep his strength. As he turns to the exit, he finds *them* waiting.

"Is this a good idea?" Cyridel asks.

"No. But do we have a choice?" Sackery returns.

"These people could use your help *inside* the city right now!"

"And who's saying that? You? Nialla's father?"

"You said the gaflings are dangerous."

"Dangerous? Yes. And more terrifying than the stories tell us."

"Are you walking to your death?"

Sackery grimaces. He stares hard at her, then at Nialla at her side. "What did you feel when it was close?" he asks her.

"Like a flood in my mind," Nialla answers. "Drowning me? Gasping for air? Pulling me down?"

"Monsters like that feed on the music that shaped the world as we know it," Sackery warns. "Singers of the Songs? Remnants of Old Eedian? Vedreron? Whatever power rules this place knows about your daughter. It will hunger after her, and she won't be safe until it's dead."

"Is it so bad as that?" Cyridel questions.

Sackery takes one large breath and exhales. "Can it be worse?" he suggests.

"I don't understand."

"Neither do I. But the Crows? They would be starving to have survived the years," Sackery admits. "Desperate? A gafling would never attack its prey outright. Powerful, but weak next to the real thing." He kneels to Nialla, wiping the hairs from her face. "They made this place their nest . . . a domain, dark and tainted."

"And you swear you can kill it?" Cyridel asks.

"I'll have to be quick and catch it—*them*—by surprise," Sackery touts. "Close the distance. Not get caught in the open."

"You're either very brave or a fool, Sackery of the Vedrethal," Cyridel denotes. "Maybe both?"

"Most likely both. Gaflings are solitary creatures," Sackery weighs. "For three to appear working together? It's hard to imagine, but it would explain everything. They make pacts with dissenters to spy on anyone who wanders too close to their lairs. It all fits perfectly in a neat little box."

"We'll wait for you to come back," Nialla says.

"Keep an eye on the wilds," Sackery pokes her nose. "I should only be a few days."

"Do you know how far you'll have to trek?" Cyridel asks.

"Depends? But you'll know when it's dead," Sackery confides. "Trust me." He stands and embraces Cyridel like a brother to a sister.

Cyridel senses the cold creeping back into the shelter when he leaves the stables. Sackery won't drop his confidence until he's far enough away that she can't pick up a flicker of what he's truthfully feeling. He's good at hiding his intentions, even when she thinks he's vulnerable.

He looks back at them from down the old forest road, eventually disappearing behind the trees.

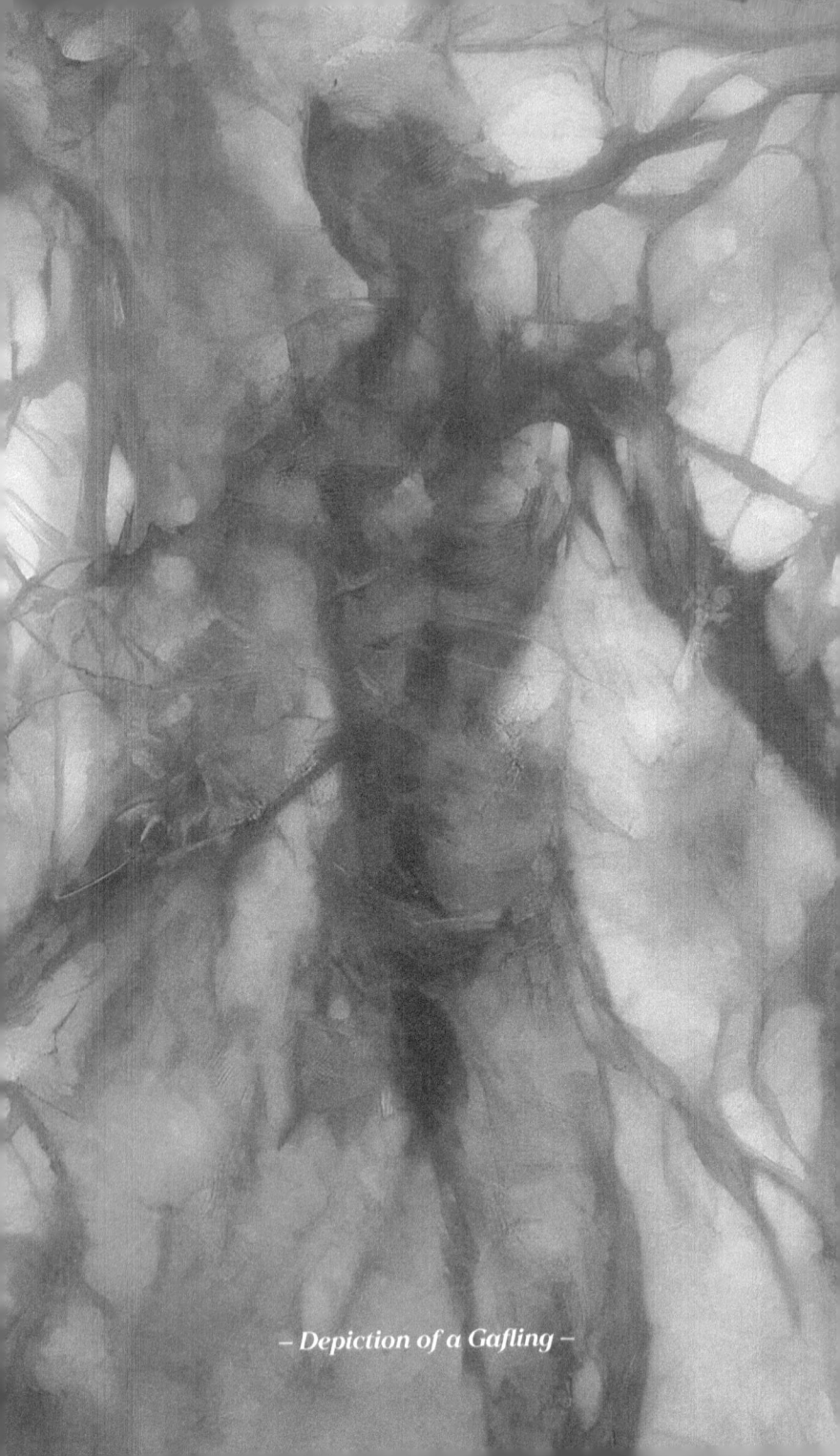

– *Depiction of a Gafling* –

— 13 —

A HOME FAR AWAY

Nialla watches Sackery leave.

It's rare for him to depart on some errand and leave them behind. And it's never left an emptiness inside like what Nialla's feeling now. He's always been there, leading the charge forward. And now? He isn't. He's gone so far ahead that she lost him in the woods.

"Only for a few days," her mother whispers.

"Then, why does this seem different?" Nialla asks.

She doesn't have an answer.

They return to the city and the tower, where so many people have taken shelter after the attack.

Yeavengeritt is there, shadows dancing across his face, light from the candles the settlers put out to ward against the night.

"I think 'foolish' is the right word to describe anyone who'd go after the Crows," the man says. "I wonder if he meant that as a comparison to—?"

Nialla's mother frowns.

Yeavengeritt notices and stops what he's about to say.

"Just beasts. Mortal," Cyridel intercedes.

"Beasts? But more than one," Yeavengeritt iterates. "Your man will learn. Trust me. What you saw out there? Those bodies and the dead? That isn't anything next to what happened a lifetime ago. That attack was a warning to stay away or acting as a lure to draw more to their deaths. I don't know which, so your friend should be cautious."

"We have faith he can do it," Nialla attests.

"Faith won't bring him back to you, little one," Yeavengeritt warns. "What if he's wrong? He will die, leaving you two alone."

"We're no stranger to bloodshed," Cyridel argues.

"But you *are* invaders in this land," Yeavengeritt follows. "I am not. It's madness out there."

"Is there anything you can do to help?" Nialla asks.

Yeavengeritt frowns. "I can assist Lord Rasterforn's soldiers with the watch tonight," he offers. "He doesn't know what to look for when the Crows' are nearby." He grasps at the door and looks back. "Always signs. First, the birds, then thunder cracks. And pain fills the mind, drowning us in fear."

Cyridel waves the man goodbye. Then, her mother turns to her.

"How's your new friend holding?" she asks.

"Scared? Like everyone else," Nialla tells her.

"Do you want to go find her? We can stay with her family tonight."

"And help reassure others that everything's fine?"

"One step at a time."

"They won't believe it," Nialla denies. "Neither do we."

"Would you rather us go after Sackery?" Cyridel asks her.

Nialla turns and stares into a candle, focusing on its little flame, making it brighter the longer she holds the gaze.

"He shouldn't have to do this alone," she murmurs.

Her mother rests her hand on Nialla's cheek, lending her a bit of warmth. She never felt cold before. But now? It's all she *can* handle, like dipping into a river, unable to come up for air. Nialla hates the water. She hates how powerless it makes her, even when she's at her strongest. She knows it follows her songs, but it is a menial adherence. It listens only to its currents, creating waves that aren't hers. For the most part, it ignores her, unaligned to either the sharp notes or the flat ones.

"Rauhnníal Badinhorn once fought a gafling and won," Cyridel recounts. "He described it as a twisted horror. Even after it was dead, the memory haunted him every night for weeks. That was before you were born. Your father had already gone off to fight in his war again. Sackery's right. It's too dangerous, even for us."

"But does he stand a chance without me?" Nialla asks. "Without each other?"

Her mother touches the chain of the necklace on her chest. She pulls it from under her clothes, a bright jewel— the Fallenstar of June. She rubs the edges like an old habit before realizing what she's doing. Nialla understands the feeling of powerlessness, wanting to draw on the familiar to make everything seem okay.

The woman who is her mother grew up in a city much like this one . . . Ilhivendal, not Trebunor. Cyridel's eyes fall to her, the daughter she never planned. A promise made between her and a father she's never known but whom everyone they meet speaks of with reverence.

Taherian Endúcar . . . Galron . . . The blue man in her dreams who followed her in the wheat fields.

It's a reminder of a world she's never seen. A life filled with love, dancing in the light. A home she will never know until she goes out and finds it.

Nialla has never had a home as her mother did. Over sixty-five years, all they did was stay on the move. She's walked ancient sites and long-abandoned ruins at the world's end, searching for something to guarantee their lives.

She's always thought it a fantasy. Something her parents kept from her, no matter how hard she tried.

"Why are we running?" Nialla asks.

Her mother looks at her with surprise. "To keep you safe."

"From enemies who likely don't know I exist?"

"It's not that easy."

Nialla grasps the jewel around her *own* neck—her father's

heirloom, the Ancestrum Stone. A rock broke on one side, the only remains of a dead man. *Where did it come from? And why?* Nialla's never had an answer, nor does she want one. It's her only tie to the man called Galron, dressed in blue, dead on the bridge after fighting the dragon, Morenarch.

Her father's battle.

She knows enough, but she also doesn't . . . Every time she asks Sackery or her mother for more, they only answer her with silence. They don't trust her to accept the truth, or they don't want to relive the memories of a man whose promise to him they kept long after his passage to Iánturial.

Is it fear that makes them cling to their trinkets?

The two stones are small things next to the gems of kings and queens. And like siblings, they share a familiar warmth.

Nialla's stone dims when she's worried and brightens when she's happy. She hides it under her clothes. But now it radiates a new light, matching *that* of Cyridel's Fallenstar. Nialla holds up her stone, watching it throb white, a dark spiral at its center.

"What's it doing?" her mother asks.

"Telling me to look outside?" Nialla begs the question.

She gets up and moves to the window. There, her mind races as she spies the white bird that appeared before the attack. It escaped the moment the slaughter in the courtyard started. *Did it want to warn them? And if it did, was the bird too late?* The bright creature takes off again, flying out of the city toward the woods.

"Shanashéron," her mother utters.

"What is it?" Nialla asks.

"A guide to the lost in dark places," she describes.

"And what does it want?"

"I don't know."

— 14 —

THE GREATER THREAT

Sackery darkly ventures. The sun reaches its peak three times and falls in cadence, meaning he left Trebunor three days ago.

He's in the Seclumor Wilds; the underbrush is sparse, the light having difficulty reaching the forest floor.

Sackery's days are spent with his eyes on the ground, tracking the footprints leading from the massacre. However, the prints are shallow, like a slender woman made them, her frame contorted with far too much space between the toes and an abnormal pressure to the heel.

At night, the camps he sets up are quaint and inconspicuous. He doesn't want the smoke to signal onlookers how to find him. Every tree surrounding him has grown to incredible and unusual shapes—branches interlocked, entangling him in a maze befitting the perverse nightmares of the insane.

"I know you," a voice speaks in the dark. *Is it a voice?* He wonders.

Sackery stops and lends his ear toward the wind. It feels like . . . it's coming from afar. But also, close by?

He looks around. "Do you know me?"

"Like a river knows its bends," the voice suggests. "Sackery of the Vedrethal?"

He notices a blurry figure wisping between the trees, an image brilliant and pure, almost like a dancer in the forest's late efflorescence.

Sackery squints, but it's like looking at something outside his vision. It's there, then it's not.

A doe comes forward from the shadows, a white coat unlike any that should exist in this wilderness. It walks into the clearing ahead of Sackery and stares at him with piercing violet eyes.

"You? Shape-changer. I saw you among the crows," Sackery remarks, looking straight at the animal. "Shanashéron? I am not lost."

"But you will not find what you're looking for without me," the other attests. "I am called Gallandhal. And I wouldn't say I was *among* the crows. They talk too much and keep no secrets. I prefer falcons—a nobler kind, courageous, and more graceful than an eagle."

"So, what? You're a doe now? A deer?"

"Sometimes. Often a hare? Or a bird? Maybe a lynx?" Gallandhal lists. "Given what we *know* lives here? I needed to hide in plain sight."

"And what *does* live here," Sackery asks, "besides my suspicions?"

"Something old? Older than the dirt, the beasts would say. It's not true, but that doesn't mean they don't like saying it."

Sackery grimaces. "Are you being vague on purpose, shape-changer?"

The doe cocks her head strangely. "Wouldn't you be?" Gallandhal returns with a shiver in her voice. She prances behind a tree, only to reappear a moment later in a different form entirely. Gallandhal is now a starkly beautiful and luminous woman with a flowing white dress draping like hair from her head. "Drastic steps to avoid their attention, Vedrethal. They live in the glade yonder those hills, the Ellúndar sanctuary called Mireaderal."

Sackery raises an eyebrow. "Mireaderal? I know the place," he admits. "It's home to another weodemair tree—Assildrusk, as I remember it." A colder breeze seeps in through the wilds as the word falls off his tongue. Even with the heat emanating from Gallandhal, it's oppressive.

"I doubt Assildrusk is as you recall him," the Shanashéron warns. "He's a gnarled thing now, left to sulk in his time as host to the Crows. The wildwoods mourn for its old keeper and that of his sibling in Trebunor. Assildrusk's leaves last fell many Autumns ago, and he's ignored Spring's onset over since."

"Gaflings leave a bad stench wherever they walk," Sackery

frowns. "Once they're dead, this land will heal."

Gallandhal shakes her head, her light dulling as if disappointed. "Gaflings? No," she shudders.

"No?"

"No," she nods.

"As in . . . not gaflings?"

"Yes."

"Then what?"

Gallandhal sinks away, afraid of the words on her mind. Sackery steps toward her, but she flinches.

"Remnants from Icurian's conflict," Gallandhal speaks. "A scornful triumvirate."

"Survivors?"

"I wouldn't say they survived," the Shanashéron mourns, her violet eyes falling groundward.

Gallandhal's heart fades to a dim light, a pain drawing on her strength. Sackery can tell, even when she looks away. There's a wound there, a story, repeating itself in these woods. But the Shanashéron is a guide in the tale, a wind that blows the grass, leading a thirsty wanderer to water.

"And how did you get involved? Why are you here?" Sackery demands.

"The same reason as you? Looking for something," Gallandhal admits. "But all I found was a trap, like a bird in a cage."

"A very large cage," Sackery submits.

"But a cage, nevertheless," the figure folds. "I can't leave."

Sackery looks hard into the woman's eyes . . . Or what eyes he *can* make out against her star-bright form.

"Okay. But three?" Sackery utters. "How did three survive alone all these years?"

"Hardly alone. *The Crows* work together," Gallandhal tells him. "You're not planning to fight them, are you?"

"Would I be here if I wasn't?" he answers with a feigned question.

"No, I don't think you would be," she accepts. "But they will kill you in the attempt."

"I've battled worse odds."

Gallandhal sputters her lips, mocking his boast. "And how much did it cost you to beat those odds?"

He shrugs. "More than I'd care to admit."

Gallandhal steps close enough to him and lays a bright hand on his shoulder. *It burns him.* "Luck can only bring you so far, Vedrethal," she whispers in his ear. "And these three? They are more connected to this land than any of the Vedr before them—Clesturia, Raenia, and Alanssia. They've bonded with every rock and branch of *their* wildwoods."

Sackery broods. "Those names?"

"You heard them before?"

"I've fought them. Years ago."

"And did you win? Against the odds?"

Sackery frowns. "Does it matter?" he returns.

"Shouldn't it? They saw your little girl," Gallandhal warns him. "They grasp what she is . . . As I do."

"Nialla is stronger than she looks," Sackery glowers.

"I—?" Gallandhal is about to say but stops as a thought breaks her words. "I didn't know her name, but she *is* like them. Nialla? I saw her with my own eyes. Yet, the Crows have also watched you since crossing the mountains." The Shanashéron musters the strength to glow a little brighter. "They *want* her. Vedreron? Something new that shouldn't exist. A child of a pact made a long time ago."

"She's the last, best chance we have," Sackery murmurs.

"And you want to protect her?" she asks.

"I'm not turning around. I won't." Sackery glares at the darkness and the centuries-neglected road. Hardly a path forward, he'll grant. But he can still follow the old markers through these ancient woods. "If what you say is true, and the Crows are not gaflings, but three of *them*, Nialla is in even more danger."

Gallandhal moves and blocks his sight. "Is it worth your life to save those sheltering in Trebunor?" she asks.

"I won't answer that," Sackery scoffs, stubborn.

"Vedrethal? Yours is a dutiful life," Gallandhal iterates. "A child who became a warrior . . . A scholar?"

"You know me," Sackery mourns, "but you don't understand me."

"No? You've spent the years correcting Icurian's mistakes," Gallandhal comforts.

"These crones are nothing but another," Sackery belittles. "They should've died years ago."

"But they didn't," Gallandhal tells him. "And now? Mireaderal is your course."

"Yes. So, it seems."

"Are you afraid?"

"Always. It's what keeps me alive."

"Then you better hope your friends are as brave as you."

Sackery looks at the Shanashéron with contempt. All she can do is nudge him away from his path. Gallandhal is a guide in a fairytale, made real by the songs that shaped the stars. Nialla is a singer of that music, as are these Crows, offering only a sour note.

Gallandhal weathered them in the years since the conflict between Icurian and Heluvian. She will do fine on her own. Sackery has never known a Shanashéron to lie. That doesn't mean he wants to hear the truth that she's spelling out for him. But through her visage, he spots the scars, the dim flickers across her body like cracks in an otherwise pristine vase.

She disappears behind him, flashing through the woods, back the way he came.

"Good luck," Sackery calls out. "Stay bright, Aerrovoshal's Child." But his voice returns to him from the emptiness.

He looks at the road ahead of him. A strong, bitter taste swells his mouth, drying his throat. Mireaderal was a Maithandír outpost built around the weodemair tree Assildrusk. A cavalry regiment had its home there, whose numbers at their height counted in the tens of hundreds. It was a safe place for travelers headed west.

Sackery once visited the site after hearing rumors that King Herranol had recalled all but a few dozen veterans to Invala Dailn. Enough to patrol the woodlands, but too few to hold it had a threat called them to action. *How old was he? Forty? Forty-five?* Older than he looked.

A different time. All it exists as images in Sackery's mind these days. Memories. Flashes, fading like dreams after he wakes.

The wilds close around him the farther he marches into the Crows' domain. *Clesturia, Raenia, and Alanssia . . .* Names he's familiar with, and in more ways than one. Like most of the Vedr, they had other labels—titles—that defined who they were, much as "Vedrethal" describes him as a warrior-servant. Names only a few like *him* still remember. But the Crows? *The Mother, the Stalker, and the Witch . . .* Monikers they took while serving Icurian in his self-styled role as Doomed King.

Sackery's hunt for them brought him to the ends of the world. He thought Icurian killed them after they betrayed his friends, *the Neshulha*, to Heluvian. Sackery shudders. His past wants to catch up to him. And if they are anything like they were, they will confront him with open arms, masking a chilling embrace.

He counts two more days until he reaches Mireaderal. That's two days to prepare for a tough fight, an end to his father's war.

– *Sackery and Gallandhal* –

— 15 —

OUR TRUE FACES

Cyridel walks the length of the wall, counting her footfalls. She glances at the woods occasionally, only to return to her meandering.

She pretends not to notice how the others look at her. They don't understand. Sackery always keeps his promises. After everything they survived together over the years, Cyridel trusts the man with her life and that of her daughter's life. But worrying for his safety isn't why she's up here now since he left four days ago. No. It's the feud in her head, weighing the chances between two sides of a square coin.

As the sun peeks over the mountains, Cyridel lets it warm her face. Even as a smokey haze dulls the light, it's enough to ward off the chilling morning air.

After a long day's vigil, she finally steps off the walls. Exhausted and drained of her strength, Cyridel wants to sleep.

She passes carts of those who died in the attack on the way to the tower. The smell is so terrible that Cyridel presses her nose to her sleeve. Rasterforn should bury them, but the only place to do so is the woods outside Trebunor's walls. And it's not safe for people to venture there. So, the bodies lay in the open for everyone to see until Sackery returns.

Inside the tower, Cyridel looks for her daughter.

"You're back?" Mrillane asks.

Cyridel glances at her. "For a time. Nialla?"

"Your girl is doing fine," Desre tells her. "She's keeping the other children busy with riddles."

"She's a clever one," Mrillane compliments.

Cyridel spots Nialla by a small hearth in the corner, talking to kids who look her age. Some older, some younger . . . They laugh despite the horror many witnessed in the courtyard. Some of their parents died then, so they are orphans with nowhere else to turn but each other.

"Who's the father, if I may ask?" Desre begs the question.

Cyridel sits down and wraps her arms around her legs. "What do you mean?" she asks.

"It isn't Master Greywolfe," Mrillane mentions. "He seems too old for you. A bit weathered in his features."

Cyridel frowns while eyeing her daughter again. *What can she say?* Nialla has never known her father. He died on that bridge, a mere whisper in her direction. Galron wouldn't have known Cyridel was pregnant. He left for the war at the Doomed King's return to lead Icurian away from Ilhivendal.

She's heard stories of what happened. And that's all she has. Stories.

"Her father was a good man," Cyridel answers. "That's all I want to say on the matter."

The two women furrow their brows at her, conspicuous.

Mrillane is the first to realize the inclination. "We are sorry," she offers.

Cyridel returns a thankful smile. "As am I," she murmurs.

"May we ask how he died?" Desre begs the question.

"It was a while ago," Cyridel tells them. "But he died in war. I can hardly remember his face."

"Do you know what they say?" Mrillane asks. "That everybody dies twice?"

"Twice?"

"The first, when the spirit leaves the body."

"And the second?"

"When those who come after you no longer remember."

Cyridel heart sinks into her chest as she warms by the candlelight, letting out an unsteady breath. As much as she hates to admit it, the woman isn't wrong. It isn't what she *wants* to hear, but it's been so long that Cyridel has to fight to bring even the smallest details about *him* to the forefront.

She looks at Nialla with the other children and smiles.

And those silver eyes? *Her* eyes? *His* eyes . . . It's one of the few reminders Cyridel still has of him. No portrait, no painting was ever made for her keepsake. Doubtless, the royal palace in Calidor will have one, but that city is the singular place where she will not bring their daughter.

That is what her father wanted, to ensure Nialla grew up as part of the world, away from the politics and schemes of his former court.

It is now the domain of his sister, Nasuria, Queen of Calidor and Greater Maheira. After Taherian died and Fredrelian disappeared, Nasuria Endúcar took up Aamelian's Throne, the mantle of the Vedreron.

"Which war did he die?" Desre asks, bumping her shoulder.

Cyridel turns to the woman. "You wouldn't know it," she tells her.

"We hear many stories in our travels. Maybe we would?"

"Leave her alone, Desre," Mrillane nudges her sister.

"Why? Aren't you curious?" Desre returns. "Look at that girl! How calm?"

"I *do* see her. But I also see how the other children act with her," Mrillane suggests. "In all our years together, have they ever been so well-behaved?" She leans forward and takes Cyridel's hands in hers. "Your daughter has a way with words, doesn't she? Her voice? Can you hear it? Like a chord that draws you in, makes you *want* to listen."

"She likes to sing her little songs," Cyridel can't help but grin proudly.

"Music to warm the heart," Mrillane joins her.

"Ankara and Nialla seem to like each other," Cyridel points out.

"My girl has always enjoyed meeting new people. But? Yes. You're right. They make fast friends."

"And *her* father?"

"Oh, he's still alive. One of the lumps hanging around downstairs."

"Soldiers have him looking over the wounded," Desre mentioned. "He's a healer. A battlefield medic and a good one."

"One of the few decent choices I've made in my life," Mrillane smiles.

"Better than me, at any rate," Desre laughingly agrees.

Cyridel chuckles, not out of pity but genuine respect for these two. They're unlike her, a princess born of bloodlines, legendary, and withdrawn. Mrillane and Desre are normal people, likely raised on a farm, judging by the callouses on their hands. Everyday folk—kind-hearted and well-intentioned, living their best lives.

As much as she enjoys these women, Cyridel sneaks away and joins her daughter.

With a blanket over her head, Nialla shows the other children by the fireside how to cast shadow puppets on the walls and make them dance. Cyridel takes Nialla's hands at one point and realizes they have no warmth, almost like a corpse. She kneels to the girl and feels her cheek. "Are you sick?"

Nialla swallows. "I'm cold. Ever since we arrived."

"Cold? You never get cold. Neither did your father,"

Cyridel worries. She looks at the kids, who all stare at them without understanding. Cyridel leads her daughter to the window, away from prying eyes. Nialla tugs on her sleeve, pointing at the rafters above them. And there, she sees it, as does everybody else in the room—a white bird with piercing violet eyes. "Shanashéron?"

The creature gawks at them, firm and illuminant. As the bird realizes it's caught the room's attention, it spreads its wings and takes off out the window. Nialla and Cyridel begin to follow the creature outside, running through the mute sunlight reflecting off the dust in the tower.

"Do you hear that? Her voice!" Nialla says. "Like a soft echo? It's beautiful."

Everyone gets out of their way as the duo hurries down the stairs. "Why the rush?" some ask.

"Didn't you see it?" a soldier laughs.

"See what?"

"The bird outside!"

"A bird?"

"Is it white?"

"A dove?!"

"No. It's too big."

"A falcon?"

"I didn't get a good look."

None of them are right. It is a Shanashéron, a guide to the lost. Most people would only know it from old stories about children in the woods running from wolves. Spotting them once was rare, but twice in a few nights? Is this the bird she saw days ago, amongst the black flock that attacked Rasterforn's people?

As they reach the courtyard, the white bird perches on the dead weodemair, drawing a crowd.

Nialla and Cyridel work around the gatherers until the creature takes off again, rising above the city.

"Where is it going?" Cyridel asks.

"I don't know," Nialla admits. "Is she leading us?"

Cyridel turns to her daughter and bumps her with her hip. Nialla laughs.

They run across the canal bridges, passing old houses, towers, and statues of beautiful lords and ladies, half-naked by the fountains. Every one of them is cracked or tarnished by neglect. Along the way, they catch glimpses of the white bird—on toppled lampposts, withered trees, and painted rocks that once were a tradition among Ellúndar cities.

A song fills the air as they go, a peaceful melody that causes everyone to look and wonder who's singing it.

It isn't long before the creature flies into a garden and disappears behind a canvas strung up by the Maheirans. Nialla and Cyridel head through the flaps, ignoring the guard's warnings to halt. Inside, the white bird lands on the central table covered with papers resembling sections of hastily drawn maps.

Rasterforn is on the far side, surprised at this strange bird suddenly confronting him in his tent, alarmed but motionless.

He looks up to greet the two at the entry and frowns:

"Would somebody like to tell me what this is about?" the man asks, not withdrawing from the bird.

The guards enter after them but do not remove the trespassers when the commander orders them to stand down.

Cyridel holds her breath. A dozen others are in the tent, scowling at the interruption—officers under Rasterforn's command. Not unlike their leader, they maintain caution toward their unexpected guests.

"Lord Rasterforn?" Nialla mutters, chilled in her tone. However, her mother can't explain why she would be.

"Commander," Cyridel follows suit, her eyes locked on the white bird in the center of the room. It bounces left and right, staring at her and Rasterforn. A brevity to its gaze makes Cyridel feel nearly weightless, like a feather. "We've been following—"

"The bird? Don't answer that! It's not a question," Rasterforn counters. "Why? I should ask." He steps around the table.

"Because I am not a bird," the creature sounds, bright enough to warm the air.

Rasterforn stops. Once more stunned, the man turns to the Shanashéron as it hops off the table. The creature lets its wings shift in a colorful display that overwhelms the candlelight in the room. His jaw drops, unable to speak.

"What are—?" Rasterforn begs the question.

The bird hops behind a pole and quickly reappears as a human female, glittering like water under the sunrise. Almost skin bare, except for a thin white dress, blurred and out of focus.

"Lord Rasterforn?" Cyridel smiles. "This is one of the proudest beings that inhabit our world."

"A white bird's feather," Rasterforn murmurs. "This can't be real?"

"You *aren't* real," the woman-form Shanashéron mocks.

"I—? I don't understand."

"Saying words, believing them? It doesn't make it true," she explains. "I am Gallandhal. And I am very real."

Cyridel looks at her daughter, whose eyes fixate on the bright, revealing shape-changer.

"I still don't—?" Rasterforn attempts to repeat. Cyridel puts a hand on his shoulder and stops him.

"There's a lot I don't understand," she comforts. "I find it's easier to accept things when they come. Fewer sleepless nights that way."

Rasterforn stares at her bafflingly. The man rubs the skin between his fingers, wringing his hands until he catches the habit.

"I can do that," Rasterforn swallows, turning to the bright creature. "Why are you here?" His confusion hardens as he confronts the Shanashéron.

"To pass along a warning to you," Gallandhal speaks. "Your friend is walking into greater danger than he will admit."

"Sackery?" Nialla spouts.

Rasterforn glances at her when she says the name.

Gallandhal surrenders a smile toward the girl. "The one called Greywolfe," she continues, "is not walking into a gafling's lair."

"No? Then whose lair is he walking into?" Rasterforn demands. "A different kind of monster?"

"The most dangerous kind. Remnants of the Old Kingdom," Gallandhal warns. "And they have names—Clesturia, Raenia, and Alanssia."

"A three-headed Crow with six wings," Nialla whispers.

"Survivors?" Cyridel finishes, gasping for air.

She catches her daughter's reaction—a spark of hope mixed with a tremoring in her knees.

"I don't understand," Rasterforn admits forlorn. "These names you speak, should I know them?"

"No. These crones were refugees that fled near the end of the war," Gallandhal describes. "Adherents of a man whose name repeats throughout history. Icurian is a name you *should* know. But they betrayed him, and he followed them here, seeking justice for their crimes. Traitors, murderers . . . faithless cravens."

Gallandhal looks at Nialla, whose eyes water, fighting to breathe.

Cyridel steps between them, only to feel a squeeze around her throat. Rasterforn and his Maheirans don't react. They don't sense it, but *she* does.

"Hold for a moment," Rasterforn orders, putting a foot forward. "Traitors, cravens, crows . . . A lot of old names for the layman's ears. And *some* names?" He looks at Nialla and Cyridel. "Older still. Sackery—? Sackery of the Vedrethal died over sixty years ago, alongside Taherian Endúcar." He keeps stepping closer to the Shanashéron. "More lies?"

Gallandhal does not retreat from her position. Instead, she shakes her head.

"You all must choose now where your loyalties lie," Gallandhal instructs, returning her attention to Nialla. "Your friend walks to his grave. Against one? He may've survived. But to fight such a threesome where Icurian once failed? He'll need your help." She lays a gentle touch on the girl's shoulder. Nialla winces as if it burns. "I warned him, and he did not listen."

"And what are we meant to do?" Nialla asks.

"Fight," Gallandhal answers, looking to the room. "All of us. Together."

"And these witches are what killed my people?" Rasterforn demands. "Are you certain?"

"As surely as the wind beats a mountain," Gallandhal confirms. "And whatever you decide? Act quickly."

"Decide? And where will you be?"

Gallandhal's form brightens. "On the road before the woods. Meet me there, and I will lead you to Mireaderal."

And with that, the Shanashéron releases a blinding light that fills the pavilion. She flies out the same way she entered, but this time, with a clear purpose.

Everyone in the tent is quiet for a long while after. The faint crackle of the candles is the only sound prevalent over the heavy breathing of soldiers in steel armor. Cyridel weighs the likelihood of them acclimating to what happened. They all heard the warning and what they must do.

Rasterforn is the first to cough. "Icurian? Vedreron, Mireaderal, Sackery," he counts, finally turning angrily at Cyridel. "Your name isn't Miralifrim. Another lie?" He signals his Maheirans to close ranks in the room. "Tell me the truth for once. All of it."

Cyridel lets out a long breath. "No. It is not my name," she confesses.

Rasterforn nods before taking a seat at the head of his table. "Remove your cloak. Show me."

She lowers her hood and reveals her ears. "I am the Daughter of Ilhivendal," Cyridel offers. "Child of Lurón and Nadrial."

Murmurs of the words "Míran" and "Ellúndar" spread fast among the soldiers in the tent. They know those names. Rasterforn's eyes meet hers again: "Like the stories I heard as a kid. You? Princess Cyridel, lover to King Taherian."

"We called him Galron when he came to us," Cyridel rectifies. "After my grandfather."

Rasterforn frowns, sitting forward for a better look at Nialla. "And this is his heir?" He asks it like she stole the wind from his lungs.

Cyridel doesn't answer. She takes her daughter's hand and

squeezes it tight.

Nialla's eyes shift a vivid, watery silver. And so now, they've shed their masks.

— 16 —

OMISSION FROM MIREADERAL

A branch under his boot snaps as Sackery puts his foot down.

The noise echoes through the trees, reverberating to him as a shiver. "An insolent child wanders into our abode," carries a voice on the wind, laughing from behind the rocks. Sackery rests his palm on the hilt of his sword and narrows his eyes. Looking ahead, he doesn't see who said it.

He steps onto the first smooth cobblestones since Trebunor, overgrown by moss and scattered leaves.

"Faithless, this one once called us," another voice comes, darker this time. "A lowly servant who feigns a love for the girl."

Sackery's limbs stiffen as he cautiously moves into the clearing.

His story is etched into his arms and armor, a Vedrethal tradition, following him wherever he goes. Burnt into the metal are figures of his past, all his hopes for the future. They comfort him even as cold vines creep across the ground toward him.

"I am a warrior-servant to the Eedian nya Ansolas," Sackery conveys to the dark empty. "Show yourselves!" He repeats the words in his head several times, demanding they answer.

"He thinks because he offends this place, he understands us?" Laughter breaks out. "He trespasses into a bad world! Our home."

"As he does. Because why not?" a third voice rings, firmer but quieter than the others. A contradiction?

Sackery closes his eyes and reaches out. It feels more . . . intelligent. Is that the right word? Stronger? As if it doesn't need to prove itself to anyone.

Those few breaths are enough to deliver the chilled hand that grasps at his throat.

Looking down, Sackery understands the history of the stones in this place. He notices the symbol linked to Enderian, the Worker, who dwelt here before the ancient Sydaunaen would call themselves Maithandír. Enderian laid the foundations these Crows now claim as their seat of power.

Cut away the surface, and the real stories reveal themselves. Mireaderal drowns in blood.

"You know me? And I know you," Sackery tells them. "Clesturia, Raenia, and Alanssia . . . Murderers turned Crows? Traitors to a betrayer."

He doesn't know how they survived the Doomed King's onslaught at the war's end. Sackery found so many bodies in his hunt for the man who adopted him, a man who attempted to undo all the wrong he did as violently as he could. Icurian betrayed Sackery and all the rest. He thought he could do the right thing but only brought death wherever he walked.

And these three? Remnants from those battles.

More lives he ruined.

Sackery bellows. "Show yourselves!" But they return only silence.

He looks at his hands and finds them trembling.

His anger won't serve him in this fight. That is obvious. Sackery takes a breath and lets it out calmly.

They will try to slow him down. Fatigue him for their final battle by chipping away his strength. He can guess because it's how Sackery fought them in the past—all those who wreaked havoc on the hard-won peace after the war with the dragons—Icurian and his followers.

Sackery stops mid-step. He reaches a meadow where all roads in Mireaderal lead. A massive tree, barren of its fruit but still alive, dominates the center dais. It imposes upon the lesser trees nearby, its limbs outstretched, casting shadows on the ground.

"Lord Assildrusk? Weodemair of the Seclumor?" Sackery asks, offering it a respectful bow.

Assildrusk's branches burr an answer: "You are not wise intruding here," the tree groans. "They demand we break you. I do not . . . want to, Vedrethal. But this valley no longer belongs to the Worker or the Ellúndar anymore. They have washed away those corpses like bloated flies on a river."

"And where are they?" Sackery asks.

"Here? There! Everywhere you look," Assildrusk burrs. "This is what they wanted, old friend."

Laughter echoes from deeper in the Wilds. "And what does a servant mutter to the slave?" it asks from nowhere.

"Assildrusk becomes reckless in its old age," another sounds. "Bygone sentience? Long forgotten."

"But which is slave, and which is the servant, Alanssia?"

"He betrays the truth he seeks, Raenia."

"Hope from the unexpected, then? An old phrase, Alanssia. Irreverent."

"An empty promise Icurian used to spout," Clesturia answers, a silhouette in the shadows. Her dress is little more than a drape, torn and worn, the threads long, rotted, and barely holding together. "And we used to listen as he spoke, a voice above voices. Icurian? Chronicler? All that dead to rights when he became the king doomed to fail."

"Does the warrior require a test? A lesson?" Alanssia puts forth. "Why else come? Not to prove his worth."

"Let's tie him down and peel the skin off his bones," Raenia seethes. "Make his fluids feed the soil. Our spiders do love it!"

Clesturia, from the dark, quiets her sisters' ramble with a solitary hand.

The other two submit, each admiring and fearful of the elder. All three sulk from the woods like predators out on a hunt.

Sackery still recognizes their faces from the last time he saw them. However, their more delicate features have succumbed to what he can only describe as rot. Their skin looks melted and sickly, scars from the battle that nearly took their lives.

Icurian . . . What did you do to them?

"Should we start him off with something familiar?" Alanssia asks her sisters. "A foe that his sword already knows?"

"And would gladly meet again," Raenia hauntingly states.

Clesturia nods, a deep frown on her face. She steps to the side with her sisters, melding with the trees.

Assildrusk shakes as drums sound across the field. Twelve figures emerge, wielding spears and shields, rusted and battered, but Maithandír in their craft. Sackery recognizes them immediately.

"What is this?" he demands. "What did you do to them?"

"We filled them with joy," Raenia laughs. "Can't you see how happy they are?"

He sees the pale of their faces, their eyes stark white. Their armor shattered into a hundred pieces, held together by ragged strips of cloth.

"Not even Icurian would do this," Sackery laments. "Tell me why?!"

"Do you truly want to know? You'll have to kill them," Alanssia mocks, a shade among the black birds watching from the tree line. "Blood tells their fates—what they are, who they were. An outrageous price, don't you think? But it's only fair, Sackery of the Vedrethal. For us! And what happened to us?"

Sackery notices more faces, maddingly carved among the underbrush, wearing masks. Wild spirits? Creatures of the woods, hewn from rock, bone, and timber.

The first thrall lunges at him with its spear aimed high. Sackery sidesteps, drawing his sword and slashing the thing across the chest. It drops to the ground, sand pouring out of the wound. "A mockery of life?" Sackery whispers, turning to the remainder. "Like dolls on strings?!" He angles the flat of his blade toward them.

"They aren't dead," Clesturia warns. "But they aren't alive, either."

"Preserved," Alanssia slithers.

"An artful expression of what good soldiers can be," Raenia laughs. "Aren't they beautiful?"

"Hideous. But all your puppets will do is slow me down," Sackery breathes. "You killed people! That can't go unanswered."

"You might as well try to beat the ocean with a stick," Alanssia mocks.

The remaining thralls move together, diligently working around him. Sackery shifts with them, always keeping the weodemair tree at his back. "You never know what's possible until you attempt it for the first time," he admits. "Surrender.

I offer you a chance."

Clesturia stands with her head tilted, amused. "How much do you remember us, Vedrethal?"

"Enough to know this wasn't always your path," Sackery answers.

"For all your life, Sackery, all you did was serve," Clesturia depicts. "You? I remember a boy on the ship—a lost cub. No mother. No father. His entire world was behind him, not knowing what was ahead. A child without a name, an outcast to outcasts."

"Icurian found me. He raised me."

"He turned you into a soldier."

"No. A killer."

"And cursed with an unnatural life," Clesturia recounts. "These thralls are *our* Vedrethal. Soldiers to spend their lives."

"These things aren't Vedrethal," Sackery denies.

"Really? And what's the difference?" Alanssia demands.

"We weren't puppets to throw against a wall," Sackery defends. "We had honor. Purpose. And most of all, each other."

"No. You were tools, discarded when broken," Clesturia argues.

"Is that what you are?" Raenia laughs.

"I stand my ground," Sackery tells them, pressing his back against the tree.

"Your legend will fail, Sackery Greywolfe," Alanssia warns

him.

"Icurian can no longer protect you!" Raenia shouts.

"He only ever protected his mad ideals," Sackery mouths, fighting their words. "I've had to chase his messes my whole life. You three are just next in a very long line. Here you are, living in the dirt with the beasts. What are you, if not leeches clinging to a carcass?"

Alanssia and Raenia hiss at him as Clestruia maintains a civil levity.

Sackery holds his sword firmly, tracking the Crows in the bushes. With the weodemair tree at his rear, he only has to guard from three sides.

"Are you not afraid to die?" Clesturia asks.

"I accepted my fate the day I took the name Vedrethal," Sackery declares.

"Then I am sorry, Vedrethal."

"You've no idea."

Clesturia returns to the dark with her sisters, and the thralls growl, answering their commands.

Eleven sand-filled husks. One dead. More in the woods, hiding in the shadows. The thralls charge at him, flailing like they don't have control over their limbs. Sackery uses the weodemair to control their approach, slipping behind it, only to reappear to poke holes in the puppets with the tip of his blade.

Three down. Nine left.

More dart forward, their spears raised high. Sackery sidesteps, getting them to miss their marks. He cuts them where their armor's broken, at the arms, the legs, the thighs . . . Anywhere his steel can find purchase, with sand coming out of them like blood. He moves fast, his sword a blur as it slices the air, humming as it stops, letting off a deathly poem.

Seven down, with five left to go.

Three flank him—two on his left, one on his right. The other two charge his front, leaving the Vedrethal boxed against the tree. Sackery angles his body, allowing the armor under his cloak to deflect their weapons, giving him enough time to riposte after parrying the attack with the flat of his blade.

It throws the puppets off balance enough for him to shove his way out of the corner.

Sackery doesn't know if the Crows intended that assault to beat him, but what it did was put him in the middle of the yard. Open on all sides.

The thralls regroup, slowly approaching him. Sackery matches their steps, wanting to keep them together but away from the woods. He glances back, feeling eyes on him from that direction. These sand-filled abominations of nature aren't the only soldiers under the influence of the Crows' black tune.

He needs to save his strength for the long haul to come.

The remainder advance in a single line, and Sackery weaves through them, barely lifting his sword. They walk into it like water on a set course. As the final one collapses, it speaks with a last breath, "Thank you." Sackery takes a moment to understand why the thralls did as they did. They were already dead men.

Sackery looks at the corpses and falls to a knee. "I am sorry," he whispers.

Clesturia approaches, her breath on his neck as she stands over him. "Do you know who they were?"

"Lords of the Seclumor. I met them. Years ago." Sackery takes a rag from his belt and wipes his blade clean.

"Ellúndar . . . Sydaunaen . . . Maithandír . . . Míran," Clesturia lists off the names. "All of them? We did this."

"You killed them."

"No. You did. We held these men to their promise."

"Promise? Is that a joke?"

"Icurian hounded us. Our mistake was asking the Lords of Trebunor for help," Clesturia tells him. "And they did, only to betray us. Left us tied for *him* to find. He kept us trapped before we clawed our way to the surface."

"They should have killed us when we threw ourselves at their mercy," Alanssia dithers. "It would've been better for everyone."

"You're the reason Icurian came this far south?" Sackery begs the question.

"You already know the tale," Clesturia refers. "One of many atrocities. Icurian sought to keep the Neshulha, the fox spirits, out of the war. Innocent beings, but with the potential to change the tide. Heluvian feared this and convinced us to find and lead their entire race to slaughter."

"You switched sides," Sackery demeans.

"We made a choice!" Raenia shouts from the woods.

Clesturia looks back at her sister and frowns. "Icurian didn't kill us," she utters.

"He was too busy running from you to finish the job," Alanssia describes.

"As he tortured us, you were hunting him," Clesturia defines. "We should thank you for that."

"I didn't do it for you," Sackery tells them.

"No. You wanted to end the war."

"He surrendered to me. I let him live!"

"Because he could never kill the boy he raised!"

"He betrayed me!"

"We're all traitors to the cause!" Clesturia screams, the woods buckling around them. "Every one of us. He wasn't the first, and we weren't the last." She circles him, the dirt under her feet cracking as she steps, the sand and leaves moving out of her way.

"You killed a city in your rampage!" Sackery calls her out with contempt.

"And how many lives have you destroyed, Vedrethal?!"

Sackery closes his fist. "Only three more?"

Clesturia draws back, surprised at how easily he said it. "Three more, and she'll be safe?"

"No. You leave *the girl* out of this," he seethes. "This is between us!"

The woman raises her head as more foes appear next to

her. "You brought a fire to a house made of kindling," Clesturia warns him, stepping behind her warrior-thralls. "Now we can fan the flames. We know *what* she is . . . Did you think we wouldn't notice? We heard her music when she entered the valley." She paces back and forth. "Today is the day Icurian's lost son learns his limits."

"You're afraid of me," Sackery realizes.

"Determined."

"You can't have her!"

"I wasn't asking."

Sackery barely lifts his sword again when more thralls fall on him. He weaves and deflects, cutting down a full score. Then, a roar comes, and his heart skips a beat. Sackery turns to the woods, realizing there's far worse than sand-filled corpses and woodland spirits under the Crows' influence.

He takes a breath as wildlings fill the gaps in the tide.

– *The Crows of Mireaderal* –

— 17 —

TO GO HOME

She reaches the bridge leading into the wilds before Lord Rasterforn catches her arm. Her mother is fast behind him.

"This is a mistake!" the man calls. "I won't allow it. Tell her it's dangerous!"

Nialla pulls her arm free with enough strength to throw Rasterforn off-balance. Cyridel sets a hand on the man's shoulder, stepping between them. A tenderness to her touch causes him to let out his breath, feeling as she feels.

"It's dangerous," she tells her. "But you don't have to follow her, my lord."

"Your friend told us to remain," Rasterforn protests. "Sackery—?"

"He's walking into a trap and needs help," Nialla explains. "Don't try to stop me. You won't."

A group of soldiers guarding the other side of the bridge

rush to join them. "No! Return to your posts," Rasterforn instructs them. "This is between us." But the fighters remain, less than willing to stay on sentry duty outside the main camp, away from the safety of numbers.

Nialla wrings her palms as they go numb.

"This is our fight, Lord Rasterforn," her mother states.

"No. Those witches killed my people," the man iterates. "This is *our* fight."

"Then gather your men and help us beat them," Nialla tells him.

"And what difference do you think it will make?" he demands. "You saw that battlefield. Would we stand a chance?"

"Probably not," Nialla admits. "But a few hundred is better than none."

"Gallandhal called us to action, my lord," Cyridel defends. "Want to call this place our home? We must first make it ours."

"But going out there? That isn't what the old man wanted," Rasterforn argues.

Nialla stomps her foot. "He wouldn't leave us! We can't abandon him."

"Sackery thought he knew the threat," her mother agrees. "He was wrong. And now—?"

"I won't let him fight this alone," Nialla states, refusing to surrender to the man, even if he *is* twice her size.

Rasterforn grimaces. "And if the Vedrethal is already dead?"

"Then I will rip the wings off those Crows and make them beg for mercy," she threatens.

Once more, the man falls back a step, off-balance. Nialla speaks the words heavily, and all the torches and candles around them brighten.

Rasterforn closes his eyes and takes another breath. He stumbles as he goes to rest on the bridge's stonework. Nialla watches him and softens her posture. She looks to her mother, who offers her an encouraging nod. She wants *her* to do this. Because if she doesn't, Sackery dies, and their idea of finding a home alongside him.

"Such big words for a little girl," the man whispers as she sits beside him.

"I am older than I look," Nialla tells him.

"But are you wiser? Maybe wise enough to know when not to fight?"

She frowns and turns away. "I don't know," she admits.

Rasterforn sits up and waves at his soldiers. They run off toward the camp, but for *what*, she can't guess.

"You want me to put my entire caravan at risk for the sake of a single man?" he asks. "A famous name or not, how do I justify it?"

"Because you're doing it to protect them."

"And what happens if we fail? Can they survive?"

"I don't know."

"Neither do I," Rasterforn murmurs.

"But what happens to them if we don't at least try?"

"We can run to the other side of the world if we need to, little one."

"And if that new place also isn't safe? Will you keep running?"

Rasterforn's shoulders sink as he hunches over his knees. "Your father? I never knew him, only heard the stories growing up," he explains. "But he wasn't invincible. He died. His tomb sits guarded in Calidor because all things must die. *You* can die." Rasterforn straightens his back and walks to the middle of the bridge. "Greywolfe? Whatever his name, he's a soldier like all the rest. Vedrethal? A warrior-servant lost to a cause."

Nialla lifts her chin. "Because they were not afraid to fight!"

"They wiped out forty men!" Rasterforn shouts. "How do you fight that?"

"I don't know! I don't know," Nialla cries. "But they will kill him if I don't do something."

"And you?! You're okay with this?" Rasterforn sneers, turning to her mother.

Nialla looks at Cyridel, noticing the tears rolling down her cheek.

She opens her mouth and closes it again, finding the courage to muster the words. "I couldn't save her father," Cyridel utters. "And when he died, I felt it. I wasn't there, but I felt it . . . the air cracked, the dragon roaring as Galron pulled the beast down and drowned it. Morenarch is dead, I heard. Taherian Endúcar is dead. And all I had of him with this little thing, cooing in my arms."

"Mama?" Nialla asks.

Cyridel meanders to Nialla and brushes a few loose hair strands behind her ears.

"My kind love only once in our lives," she mourns. "It's a promise we make to each other. Unbreakable."

"And after that? You ran?" Rasterforn asks.

"Sackery found us. Told us what happened," Cyridel explains. "Galron made him promise. He said that others would hunt our daughter for *what* she is, *who* she is . . . He wanted us to keep her hidden, no matter the cost. And for sixty-five years, we ran until our feet bled, and we lost ourselves in this massive world."

"Just two faces amongst the crowds?"

"Is there a better way to hide?"

Rasterforn lends his weight to one foot and crosses his arms. He studies the two of them. "No."

Nialla notices the muscles in his jaw clench after he speaks.

A large group of soldiers returns to the bridge, arriving from the Trebunor encampment. Rasterforn joins them, whispering to one of the officers.

Nialla turns an ear, but she can't determine what the man's telling them.

"Am I understood?" Rasterforn finally says loud enough to hear.

"Yes, Lord Commander," the lead woman answers.

"Good. Make ready the spears, Fianna," Rasterforn orders. "Prepare for a hard march. We leave within the hour!"

"You're coming with us?" Nialla asks.

"We'll do what we must," he lowers his head to her, "and protect what's ours."

"You're not afraid?" Cyridel begs the question.

"Terrified."

"And your people know what they're walking into?"

"They'll learn soon enough," Rasterforn admits. "Sackery has four days on us."

"Gallandhal will take us on the quickest path," Cyridel contends.

"But we aren't only going to be following the bird," Rasterforn decides, looking at Nialla confidently. "Can you do this?"

"I will try my best," Nialla answers.

"Your friend's life is on the line, little one," Rasterforn consoles. "He'll need more than 'try' from you."

"I'll get us there," Nialla stands her ground.

Rasterforn pounds his chest once in acknowledgment before jaunting across the bridge to the camp.

Nialla collapses into her mother's arms, who carries her aside. She can hardly breathe, and the chill in her bones comes from all directions now.

"Are you okay?" her mother asks.

"It's like somebody's pressing down on my chest," Nialla tells her.

"Somebody?"

"I don't know. Their hand's cold."

Her mother squeezes her and kisses her on the head. "It'll be all right," she says.

"How do you know that?"

"I don't. But I have faith we can make it work."

"It feels like something is cutting me."

"Close your mind to it. Or think of something happy to fill the space."

"Happy?"

"Maybe a song?" her mother offers. "Remember the lullaby I used to sing to you?" She allows Nialla to stand on her own.

"The one about dreams and mountains?" Nialla asks.

"No. Well, maybe? Those are certainly some of the words," Cyridel describes. "My mother sang it to me as a girl on cold and lonely nights. And I can only assume my grandmother sang it to her when she lived with the Aens."

"I remember. Can you sing it to me again?"

"For as long as you need me to, I will. Do you want to start?"

Nialla smiles before she breathes. "And you'll dream."

"Of a world you have never seen," Cyridel recants.

"A life of love and dancing in the light."

"Beyond the ranges stand."

"A home you've never known."

Nialla stares at her mother as the song fills the air, starting weak and uncomfortable. But then, their words grow with force, and the breeze quiets to a meager sputter that barely moves the trees on the other side of the bridge. Nialla rests her chin on her mother's shoulder as they hum the final verses.

"Let these words brighten your world when it is darkest," Cyridel whispers in her ear.

"Thank you," Nialla weeps.

"Never forget where you come from, my little sprite."

— 18 —

CRIMES OF THE PAST

Sackery drops to his knee after slashing the beast across its throat. He doesn't even know *what* monster it was . . . A malformed boar? Blood trickles from his nose, running down to his chin. He's lost count of how many are dead on the field.

More approach. Sackery pushes off the ground, but his legs fight him.

"He is tired," Alanssia utters.

"But still resilient," Clesturia realizes.

"After two days, how is that possible?" Raenia demands.

The crones walk into the clearing from the shadows. Clesturia stops beside him, fascinated by this boy Icurian raised as a son and weapon. Sackery tries to swing at her with his blade, but the woman steps out of the way faster than he can lift his arm.

"He is a warrior," she adds. "All he knows is the fight."

Sackery counts the scars on her face, like pieces of glass melded together by pouring gold into the cracks.

"I should have let Icurian finish what he started with you three," Sackery weeps.

"Questions of what 'should have' been don't matter," Clesturia refuses. "All that matters is what 'will be' for us."

Sackery raises his head and looks into her eyes, dark and full of century-old pain.

"I don't know what you mean," he feigns ignorance.

"We don't believe you," Raenia laughs.

"Quiet!" Alanssia calls her sister out. "Let them talk."

Clesturia looks back at them before returning to Sackery. "Why did you bring the girl here?" she bluntly asks.

Sackery attempts to stand again, but his armor is too heavy. And even if he could, the Crows wouldn't risk themselves by getting too close. Not when they have an army of thralls to throw against him. He can hear them in the trees—the beasts, the puppets, and the gnarled woodland spirits. And *one* among them, more powerful than the rest. A massive bear that stalks the perimeter, bark-like hide, its limbs like great trunks.

He knows its name, its anger causing the trees to shift. A forest guardian, forced to serve these twisted masters.

The Mórhathan.

"We were looking for you," Sackery tells them—a lie and not a very good one.

"Icurian was never good at lying," Clesturia calls him out.

"Obsessive truth-teller, he was," Raenia recalls. "Even after his fall, he was always honest with his enemies."

"He told us *honestly* how we were going to die," Alanssia explains. "Buried us alive. A lie would have been comforting."

"Doubtless, you inherited the habit," Clesturia mocks.

All three circle him like predators to wounded prey, their eyes red and violent. But they are patient for keeping him alive this long, despite appearances. He looks at the dead thralls littering the ground around the weodemair tree. Hundreds? Enough to turn the tide of a battle.

"I remember very well," Sackery tells them. "A king's ungraceful decline."

Clesturia slows her stride as she throws him a waterskin. "Icurian was your enemy," she says, letting him drink. "Across the years, how many battles did you fight? You loved each other once, father and son. But no matter what you two did to one another, that love never waned. That's why you couldn't strike a killing blow. You failed, Sackery of the Vedrethal. So much could've been different."

"Another trait I inherited from him," Sackery mocks. "I am bad at what I do." He wipes a trickle of water from his mouth.

"Then why bring her to us?" Alanssia issues.

Sackery lets off a confident smirk. "Is that what you think I did?"

"Vedreron? A half-breed, abomination of a little girl," Raenia describes. "An insult against the natural order!"

"Much like what you three have done to this valley?" Sackery accuses, pulling at his limbs. "Don't flatter yourselves. We didn't know about you until you attacked those settlers at Trebunor!" He finds his legs, mustering the strength to raise his sword again. "This had nothing to do with you until you became a threat."

Each of the three stops circling Sackery and takes a cautious step closer to him.

Clesturia is the clever one . . . Her offering him water was a plan to see how near the edge they had him. Raenia is a madwoman, cackling every time she opens her mouth to speak. Icurian broke her mind if not her spirit. All while Alanssia remains . . . somewhere in-between . . . a low cunning, yet powerfully unpredictable on which side of the coin she'll land in a straight fight.

"You can't keep going at us as you are, Vedrethal," Clesturia warns him.

"Maybe. But I played this dance before," Sackery returns. "You three aren't very good at it."

"We took this place and made it ours!" Raenia shouts.

"You are the trespasser!" Alanssia joins her sister. "Everything here answers to us!"

"Do you believe that?" Sackery calls them out. "No. We're in a nest of dead things. You live in squalor!"

"Is that a taunt?" Clesturia seethes. "This is our place. Our sanctuary."

"Then step closer," he dares them. "Defend it! Let me show you the killer I am."

Raenia charges at him, taking the bait like a moth to the flame. Sackery draws back and stops her with the point of his blade, advancing in cadence. Clesturia steps between them, knocking his sword out of his hands. She's fast, almost too fast for him to react. He ducks out of the way and tries bringing her down at the knee.

Clesturia lowers a hand and throws him into the dirt.

It knocks the wind out of him. Sackery coughs blood, wiping it off with his sleeve.

He can fight on no longer. That was the last he could muster.

"You are parasites," Sackery says. "Nothing more."

Clesturia looks down at him, not saying a word. She nods to her sisters, and thralls come with chains, wrapping them around his arms and torso. They drag him across the field to a boulder under the weodemair's great branches. Sackery can hear the sentient tree groan as it sits and watches him be shackled.

"We cleaned out the parasites," Alanssia returns. "You are the last."

"As will be your little girl," Raenia sneers.

"Don't—" he coughs. "Don't you go near her!"

Alanssia closes her fist, the chains tightening around Sackery's wrists. "Or what?" she asks.

"Her song echoed when you came over the mountains," Clesturia glowers, stopping before him, bending down until he can smell the rot on her breath. "Her footsteps hit like thunder on the rocks. All those years you spent fighting Icurian's rebellion, did you ever learn how we hear each other?"

"Your songs shaped the land and sea," Sackery murmurs. "Of course, I learned."

"And in Trebunor? She brought a new tune," Clesturia utters. "I heard it!"

"Brighter than the sun on a warm day," Alanssia commits.

"Enough to breathe life into a small flower that wilted decades ago," Raenia finishes, hardly a chuckle in her voice.

Sackery pulls on the chains that leash him to the rock. "She shouldn't have done that."

"Why not? It was beautiful," Clesturia adulates.

"And we thank you for bringing her to us," Alanssia agrees.

Sackery looks at the sisters, each of them frozen in time. They appear in so much pain, the scars on their once-perfect faces. How do they even stay upright? Leaves fall from the treetops, stopping where the air is motionless, a barrier dividing the thralls chattering in the dark spaces beyond the Weodemair's Grove.

Assildrusk shakes violently as if a chill is crawling down its limbs. Is it the cold? Or a warmth that makes everything else seem colder. A dull light from the woods outside Mireaderal's holdings shows itself . . . It breaks through the trees like the sun after a rainstorm, blinding like some distant fire, white as the stars.

A sharp metallic hum fades into a hazily familiar voice.

Sackery grunts. There's a moment when the man hears a ringing in his ears, drowning his remaining senses like he's underwater.

He looks up and marks the source, smiling with renewed confidence.

"Do you remember the story they used to tell us about when the Vedr fell from Anánturial and woke up to a young world?" Sackery questions, naming the heavens where those like Icurian, Heluvian, and indeed, Clesturia, Alanssia, and Raenia were born.

"Of course, we remember," Clesturia tells him.

"Icurian told me of those early days," he continues. "All he went through with Heluvian, two brothers who fought the darkness together, now lost somewhere the light had only begun to touch. A broken tree branch and a rock from high above were all they had, floating amidst crashing ocean waves. Stranded." Sackery notices the Crows' eyes dilate.

"They did eventually find their way to shore with the rest of us," Alanssia describes.

"But they were weak," Sackery corrects. "And their powers, all your powers, diminished,"

"Why speak of this?" Clesturia demands. "We lived it, Vedrethal."

"Yes. And drifting in the water, Heluvian and Icurian didn't find their way by themselves," Sackery coughs. "An eagle visited them at their most desperate hour. The bird perched itself on the branch, not knowing more than a bird ought to know. It couldn't speak, nor did it understand the Iírdun tongue."

"Icurian still had the broken-off fragment from our home," Clesturia realizes. "He allowed the bird to take the stone in its beak, a light in the dark."

Alanssia snorts, drawing too close to him. "It granted the creature intelligence and the power to change its form at will."

"Hope from the unexpected," Sackery chants.

Clesturia eyes him with disgust. "And what's the point of telling us this?"

Gallandhal nods to Sackery from high in the trees, the three unaware of the bird's presence.

"Because since then, the Shanashéron and Vedr share a close bond," Sackery answers. Blood fills his mouth. He can taste it on his lips as he speaks. "That eagle's name was Aerrovoshal. And it is said wherever the Vedreron are, or their descendants, a white bird is never far behind."

Sackery knew *she* wouldn't abandon him.

– *Sackery defends against the onslaught* –

DAUGHTER OF THE MOUNTAINS

She collapses against a tree. With every step she takes, the weight bears down on her. She's tired now. How is she tired?

Her vision blurs and darkens. She notices Gallandhal watching her from the trees, a white bird in a sea of black. Nialla feels the warmth radiate from the creature, keeping the cold from breaking through and swallowing her whole.

Rasterforn rides up next to her on the trail. "What's the matter?"

Nialla takes a breath. "We're almost there," she frowns.

"Almost?" he asks, looking out over the woods, his mare tugging on its reigns. "You're pale. Can you stand?"

The wind shifts direction, causing the branches above them to shift violently.

"I don't know," Nialla admits.

Rasterforn lowers a hand to her. "Here! You need to rest,"

the man offers. "We can take you."

Nialla doesn't accept it, not at first. She looks at the horse, its snout digging into her head, smelling her hair.

"What's her name?"

"Ryallamere."

"Hello there, Ryallamere," Nialla whispers to the mare, brushing its silver mane.

The animal stands proud, its grey coat reflecting the trace sunlight that breaks through the forest canopy. Nialla laughs as Ryallamere licks her cheek.

"Can you stand now?" Rasterforn asks.

Nialla takes his hand. "I can try."

"You don't have to go at this alone," Rasterforn tells her. "There's no shame asking for help."

"It's not that."

"Then what is it?"

"I can hear them. Their voices," Nialla utters. "They've hurt him."

Rasterforn eyes her with a forlorn hope. "I only hear the wind," he cautions.

Nialla closes her eyes and lends an ear to the breeze. It's soft, like a hum, floating in the air. Stark rumbles and groans as the trees whisper to each other, with only *her* name repeating in their laborious speech. Nialla's breath shortens as she reaches out, the muscles in her arm cramping as something squeezes her heart.

Rasterforn's brows scrunch together, looking at her and

noticing the obvious.

"And what are the trees saying?" he begs the question.

Nialla lets out her breath. "To stay away," she reads, a tingling on her fingertips.

She hops on top of Ryallamere and finds her place in the saddle. Nialla doesn't know how to ride a horse, so she holds onto Rasterforn's waist as he canters to the front of the marchers. Seven hundred soldiers, riders, and footmen clump down the old forest road from Trebunor to Mireaderal.

The air thins as they go, burning her throat and making it hard for Nialla to stay awake. Black birds covet the trees, watching the army as they pass under, telling their secrets. The witches know she's here without a doubt.

"It's not safe to linger," Nialla tells Rasterforn.

"You see them, too?" he asks.

She looks up as Gallandhal sweeps the trees, scaring the birds off their perches.

"They wonder who is going to win," she notions.

"Are these entire wilds loyal to the crones?

"Maybe? I don't think the creatures have had much choice."

"Creatures?" Rasterforn begs the question.

"Woodland fairies, beasts, shadows, and darker things," Nialla describes him. "All things to scare children from the woods."

"This is their home," he realizes.

"These trees are ancient," she whispers mournfully.

"You can hear them speak to one another?"

"Their songs call out in praise and fear."

"Fear of us?"

"For us, my lord. These wilds are a cage, and we are walking into it."

"We'll fight for this place to become our home."

"But for now, it is the Crows' home, and we are only trespassers."

She looks back at the soldiers in the column. Her mother's there, walking in sight, never taking her eyes off Nialla.

In her mother's world, in Ilhivendal, children learned more than any human would in a lifetime. Listening to the stories, Nialla imagined those dancing silver waters in white-stone fountains, waiting under lordly statues, naked in the sunlight as the morning dawns.

Trebunor and Mireaderal used to resemble that, she is certain. Nialla understands those proud days are gone for the world's oldest places. There's no turning back the centuries to fix everything that went wrong. "No returning the dead to life," as her mother said, "from a thousand years ago."

They push into Mireaderal's ruined depths. Voices urge her onward.

She shrugs them off, refusing to listen. The trees dig deeper into the dirt as the conflict between Nialla and the Crows reaches a cadence, snapping at the air and cracking stones as they pass. A wind comes to knock the riders off their horses.

Rasterforn helps her dismount and joins the others in raising their shields.

"What's happening?" he asks.

"I've never seen a storm like this!" a soldier calls.

"Why are we following this girl into the thick of it?" another asks.

"This is a bad omen!"

"Can anybody see where we're going?"

Rasterforn doesn't answer them. *What can he tell them?*

They didn't have to follow her into the wilds, but they did. Nialla sorely wished they hadn't. It'd be safer.

"Stay together!" Rasterforn orders. "Overlap those shields!"

Nialla gets shoved between the ranks, her mother nowhere to be seen. The metal of the soldiers' armor stings as she gets pressed against it. Frost cumulates on the leaves and bushes along the trail. Her tears freeze on her cheeks. All her life, Nialla had never once felt cold. And in days, she's learned why her parents hate it.

"We need to keep moving!" somebody shouts.

"The wind's breaking hard on us! How do we push?"

"We step together!"

Nialla feels a jerk as the Maheirans advance against the incoming gales. But it blows harder against them, fighting them. Rasterforn and his men brace themselves and find their footings before making another attempt. They lock shields and arms, stepping like a single mechanical beast, trading momentum for chances to catch their breath.

It's all they can do to keep this force from overtaking them.

Nialla musters her strength, breaking free of the pack. She

runs ahead of them and toward the trees.

Rasterforn attempts to grab her, but she wiggles out of his grip. "Girl! What are you doing?"

"The only thing I can do!" Nialla shouts back.

The wind slows her steps, but she drives hard against it, cutting through the chilling air. She clenches her jaw, draws back, reaches out, and rips the wilds apart. Splinters fly everywhere, and the world darkens to an empty black void. Everything disappears . . . the woods, the soldiers, the very sky above her.

All left is the level pool of water cusping the top of her boot.

What did she do? Where is she? How did—?

There's a clearing ahead, alive with a grand old tree, gnarled and fat—a weodemair, larger than the dead one in Trebunor. It presides over the central dais with a grim, defeated hum. Its branches hang low, too sullen to bother reaching for sunlight.

"Hello?" Nialla asks it.

The great tree burrs slightly and shakes its branches. "You should not be here," it warns.

"I am not going anywhere," she tells it. "I am looking for somebody."

"And he is here," another voice says, almost laughing at her.

Nialla turns. Sackery is bound in chains to a rock near the field's far side. His muscles convulse. His eyes shine a brilliant blue despite the blood on his face.

Bodies lay everywhere, still in the void—bodies of men, boars, wolves, and creatures she'd only heard stories about.

The black slowly fades away, and the woods rebound to a clear view.

The wind cracks through the clearing as the Crows gather around the old Vedrethal.

"What are you?" one of them demands.

The tallest of the three steps forward. "Something new? You?" She tilts her head. "Such a small creature to stomp so loudly."

Nialla opens her mouth, but she does not answer.

"And look at that! She's brought friends," the third laughs.

Looking behind her, Nialla can see Rasterforn alone marching into the meadow. He doesn't speak. No. All he does is offer Nialla a nod, worn but determined.

She smiles and swallows. Nialla turns back to the Crows and Sackery in his chains.

"We came for him," Nialla speaks. "What did you do to him?"

"We tried teaching him respect," Raenia answers.

"Sackery of the Vedrethal is a slow learner," Alanssia adds.

"Or you're just a bad teacher," Sackery chuckles.

The crones look at him with amusement. "And still with the bad manners," Clesturia returns.

Nialla studies them. Sackery fought to the point of exhaustion.

"Let him go," she demands.

"What was that?" Raenia cackles.

"I believe she told us to let him go," Alanssia issues.

"You have no influence here, little seed," Clesturia denies. "This land is ours. As is everything our songs touch."

Rasterforn comes alongside Nialla, squeezing her arm. "No. You stole it," he decides, his foot soldiers joining the field.

The tall one laughs, measured but obvious as a way to mock him.

"We laid our claim. Nothing more."

"The people here denied us. Fought us."

"And we won."

Rasterforn shakes his head. "You killed my people!" he argues.

"Yes. We did," Clesturia admits.

"We did nothing to you," Rasterforn swallows. "Why did you? Those men had children!"

"They were in our way," Alanssia tells him unapologetically.

A warm tinge graces the back of Nialla's neck. Gallandhal is above her in the trees, watching everything on the field below. Rasterforn and his soldiers draw their weapons—spears, and shields—forming a defensive wall along the outer dais.

"I loved all those people, their families," Rasterforn barks. "Some walked with me since Calidor."

Clestruia raises her hand, urging her sisters to back away. Alanssia, the middle one, bows her head and quickly fades into the woods. Raenia, the smallest but the most scarred and fierce, hesitates a moment longer before following her.

"And can you do with so few," Clesturia asks, "what a thousand couldn't do? If you had tracked a buck to its lair and killed it before its fawns, you'd still have skinned the animal and debated whether to do the same to the young."

"We are not animals," Rasterforn protests.

"Maybe not," Clesturia returns. "But to survive? Even a great man fears hunger."

"You have no more friends to call on," Raenia laughs in the dark.

"You are alone with only a girl to defend you," Alanssia joins her in the threat.

"Alone to fight the terrors that stalk these wilds."

"Where wits and strength are meaningless."

"Where survival means everything."

"And death is never the end."

"Do you understand?" Clesturia demands. Her eyes land on Nialla, only a meager light shining through the trees. "For every step you took in the mountains? We felt it. For every breath in the clouds, the whispers around the campfires, the tears at night as your thoughts linger on a home that could someday be yours? We heard it all like you were next to us, little one."

"You knew I would come," Nialla whispers.

"You've come seeking war," Clesturia speaks, powerful in her tone. "That leaves an impression that's difficult to hide."

"And this is a war you cannot win," Alanssia finishes, unseen.

Nialla frowns before stepping ahead of Rasterforn and his soldiers. "I don't care," she mourns, looking at Sackery, chained and beaten.

"We'll fight it anyway," Rasterforn declares.

Clestruia recedes into the Wilds, where a virtual flood of enemies step inward to take her place with blood-curdling war cries. From those streams, shadows form into vaguely man-like shapes—flesh and blood—a glazed, empty look in their eyes. They surge forward against Rasterforn's battle line like water on a stony shore. Steel and shields clash hard as spears break, and arrows *whish* through the air and pierce rusted armor with a dozen hollow thuds.

Rasterforn throws Nialla behind him, buffering her from a blow that splinters his shield.

"Get back!" he yells. "I can handle—"

"We have to push toward Sackery!" Nialla points as the man battles.

Rasterforn looks up to see Sackery still tied where the Crows left him, bleeding on the other side of the field.

"He's the bait!" he decries. "They want us to push!"

"No! He's the prize. They are afraid of him."

"And what can he do that we can't?"

"He can kill them!"

The man pushes some beast off him, looking at her with teary eyes. Rasterforn warily nods and signals for his cavalry to emerge from the woods and charge into the opposing force. They knock a great mass of their enemies aside. These aren't men. Real soldiers could take an attack on that scale and hold the line.

But these things? The crones employ specters from the forest, dead as much as they are alive. They move with all the fury of their mistresses—mindless and savage, not caring for their well-being. Unlike the Crows, survival doesn't mean anything. They are sent into the fray to die, so that is what they are doing.

Nialla yelps as she's thrown to the ground and trampled.

She covers her head and crawls when nobody notices. A man drags her to her feet, pushing her in the right direction.

Rasterforn and his men cut through the field, only for more thralls to swarm from the dark woods to replace the ones that fall. Hundreds . . . A thousand? Bodies crashing on bodies, battle-harden men screaming at the top of their lungs, crying out as some are torn from their armor and pulled apart. Horses mewl as their riders get knocked off and escape into the woods.

She hears the animals dying as something catches them.

The Maheirans, in a desperate attempt to stem the tide, regroup near the center of the field under the weodemair.

Rasterforn orders them into a circle, filling the gaps left after the assault.

Alanssia and Raenia remain on the outer edge, ripping through bone and steel as if arms and armor were parchment paper.

Her mother, with scrapes on her hands and legs, finds Nialla. She was in the middle of the heaviest fighting, helping pull the wounded to safety behind their lines.

"You shouldn't have come," Rasterforn argues under his breath. "They wanted us to find them."

Nialla stares at him, baffled. "We never stood a chance."

She covers her eyes as the battle renews, hiding by the tree. The weodemair moans and vibrates as a branch reaches down and touches her cheek, and all the color of the world fades into that empty void she was in before. All that remained were the tree, the Crows, Sackery, and the bloodwater at her feet.

It is what she saw when she looked into Yeavengeritt's mind. She doesn't understand.

"Where am I?" she asks.

Clesturia steps toward her with a dull grace. "Where do you think we are?"

"You pulled me into some vision . . . some darker worldly aspect."

"We have many powers, but illusions were never our strength, little one."

"Then, what is it?"

"This is our mind space," Clesturia answers. "Our shared connection."

"All so we may speak freely to one another," Alanssia explains.

"Without distractions," Raenia mourns.

Nialla looks at them, no longer the damaged faces of once beautiful women. They now appear bright, full of life, and as young as the first blossoms on a cherry tree. Their dresses flow like they are part of the wind, as light as air but made of dust, disappearing into the black as the cloth flies.

"And why am I here?" Nialla demands.

"To offer you a choice," Clesturia tells her.

"This isn't real," she returns.

"But it does feel real, doesn't it?" Clesturia wonders, walking through the blood sea. "Every aspect of it—the red water at our knees to the air we inhale. All are very lifelike. Not an illusion, but how we choose to see the world, and how it deserves notice."

Nialla takes a breath. She can smell the sweat of the men around her outside this vision.

"You can't mask the stench," Nialla refuses to believe.

Clesturia tilts her head to one side. "No. We can't," she admits.

"And it's too small."

"We are under an open sky. How is it too small?"

"Because I have lived under the sky my entire life," Nialla explains. "This feels confined."

"A noteworthy contradiction," Alanssia suggests.

"Unless she is only talking to buy time," Raenia rejects.

"And what about the sound?" Clesturia urges. "Can you hear your friends dying?"

Nialla closes her eyes and focuses . . . But the noise is a

muffle, a quaint droplet falling into a vast ocean. Enough to cause ripples, but they quickly scatter on the surface, unable to break through the veil between the outside and the Crows' deserted imagination.

She closes her hand around the gemstone at her neck.

"They are still fighting," Nialla utters.

"Yes. And soon, your friends will die. As will your mother," Raenia threatens.

"Leaving you alone in the world with nobody but *us* to teach you," Alanssia offers.

Clesturia holds out a hand. Nialla swallows.

"Leave her alone!" Sackery coughs, mustering the strength to pull his chains.

"Or what? Son of Icurian," Alanssia taunts.

Sackery struggles to raise his head. "Icurian was once a hero to every man, woman, and child under the sun," he describes. "People flocked. Wiser scholars than I have asked why so many followed him after the darkness took hold. Folk wanted to remember the man he was, not what he became, the husk of a doomed king."

"You saw through his heroic mask, Vedrethal," Clesturia denotes. "Stood your ground."

"But look at what he did to *us* once we saw past his words?" Alanssia issues.

Clesturia turns back to Nialla under the weodemair tree. "And what would you do, little one, had our fates been different?" She melds with the black void, like an image through glass, her face flickering between the beautiful and the scorned.

"We can add your voice to ours!" Alanssia suggests.

"Make our songs spread far and wide," Raenia echoes.

"Correcting the injustice done to us," Clesturia speaks, stepping out of the dark with her sisters. "Do you see the road ahead? It is your choice."

"And what a fate it is, should you choose incorrectly," Alanssia adds.

"Will you walk the sunken road?" Raenia wonders.

"Or will you die here with the rest of these people?" Clesturia demands.

The stone around Nialla's neck warms as she squeezes it. She hears it buzz, like a wheat field in the sun, with the bugs and birds chirping on a summer's afternoon. It reminds her of the wonderful lullaby her mother sings, like seeing a child playing in the water. And with it, an old memory crops up from when they stayed at a farmstead in a faraway land. Nialla doesn't remember the place's name, but the music lingers, not sung by her mother this time.

A man dressed in a blue cloak was overlooking her crib. His fingers danced around her nose. It wasn't Sackery. Or anybody else whose name she remembers.

Nialla tried to grab his fingers, but the man pulled them away, laughing as he did so.

Is it a reflection from when she was still a baby? Or is it a trick by the Crows to play with her mind?

Nialla takes a breath and releases it, warming the air and causing the world's color to break through the black. She hums it louder until finally letting the song loose, exactly as the man sings it in her memory:

And you'll dream,
Of a world you've never seen,
A life of love and dancing in the light,
Beyond the ranges stand,
A home you've never known.

Your heart,
Is bound for more, my dear,
A power your blood adorns,
Beyond the river's rise,
A fate never meant as yours.

But you'll stand,
Apart the world where towers,
Are falling down, beyond,
The valley heights,
Of a past you shall never know.

And you'll rise,
To the open fields afar,
A kingdom of stone and ash,
Beyond the mountain swells,

To a life you have never known.

The Crows drop back, startled by the onslaught of the song in their fortress.

It's enough for this dream-like state to break . . . Shatter it like glass! Nialla will not allow herself to be captive like Yeavengeritt was for centuries! She wakes with a breath that causes all the trees in the field to rise and shut out the twisted chords the Crows have whispered to them for all these years.

And as the black fades away, the sound of the battle escalates around her.

Nialla unexpectedly finds herself standing over Sackery, his chains in her hands, broken and free. She doesn't remember walking to him, but she did. And he looks at her with such pride that all she can do is smile before her legs give out and she collapses.

She made her choice.

— 20 —

BATTLE OF LOST PROMISES

Sackery catches the girl as she drops, dragging her away from the battle.

Every muscle in his body clenches in pain. Sackery bites down on his molars, fighting to keep Nialla's head off the ground. He doesn't know what happened between her and the Crows and doesn't need to know. Sackery had ordered her to stay put and wait for him in Trebunor. She came anyway.

He lays her against a tree. "Why couldn't you leave it alone? Stubborn girl."

The battle rages around them in effluvium—dust and soil kicked up, blood collecting in the footstones, and running in pools like a creek after the winter's thaw.

Lord Rasterforn and his troops hold their line in the middle of the field. He musters his fighters and pushes toward the flanks, luring the thralls into a killing zone in the center, where the archers pick off stragglers as bodily waves clash with the spear wall.

Assildrusk—the weodemair tree—shivers as a mist seeps in from the surrounding woods, and every damp surface turns to a thin, icy layer. Clesturia, Alanssia, and Raenia press hard against Nialla's defenses. And like a good girl, she pushes back. It is the physical embodiment of their struggle, their minds colliding in whatever dark space fills their dreams.

"You're okay. It's all right," Sackery whispers to Nialla. "I'm not leaving you. Not here. Not ever."

Tears roll down her cheeks. He cleans them off with his sleeve and kisses her forehead. Her entire body shakes.

Sackery finds an abandoned sword from the dirt and cuts down thralls that dare come near her. Myheirad, his sword, vanished. Likely, the Crows took it away when Clesturia snapped it from his hands. He doesn't know where it went. Sackery's wielded that blade for his entire adult life—across eons. It was a part of him, like his arm. But he doesn't need it to fend off these foes.

An ancient guardian spirit of the woods takes the field— bark-like hide and massive in size—a kindred beast to the wild ones that roam these lands, primal in its temperament. It roars and charges, attacking Rasterforn's soldiers and the Crows' thralls.

Sackery knows the Forest Guardian by its ancient name— the Mórhathan. And it does not fight for anyone's side.

It fights for itself, to defend itself and the wildwoods.

"Treacherous beast!" one of the Crows shouts.

"Look out!" Rasterforn calls, pulling his troops back to the weodemair tree.

"It's on a rampage!"

"Shore up the left flank!"

"Brace your spears! Hold the line!"

"It's broken through the enemy's ranks!"

"Don't fight it!"

"Retreat!"

Sackery breathes, rattled and exhausted. He's fought a hundred battles and killed thousands in his lifetime. But this may be the first time he loses if he can't find a way to turn the tide.

He looks down at Nialla, unable to get up and join him.

Cyridel is with Rasterforn by Assildrusk, helping the wounded escape the carnage and protecting them as the line collapses.

Sackery readies his sword and fights on, avoiding the Mórhathan where he can. He draws thralls away from the Maheirans. At certain moments, it's as if the creature and the man are fighting together against a common foe. However, only if Sackery ignores the beast's occasional swipe at his throat when he draws too close. Yet the Mórhathan's presence unmistakably turns the battle against the Crows. Sackery can hear the sisters wail as they send more of their slaves to the slaughter.

And that is when he doesn't lose track of the beast. Sackery turns and finds it lumbering toward Nialla, where he left her.

He holds his breath, gripping the hilt of his sword tight. Sackery prepares to charge the creature and force it away from the girl. But he doesn't. Nialla sits up as the Mórhathan smells her hair, cooing her like it would its cubs. She rests her hand on its snout, and *it* lets her. Without a doubt, the creature rubs its nose against her cheeks, grunting as if speaking a language only Nialla understands.

That's when the Mórhathan turns and roars loud enough to shake the trees. All eyes in the field look suddenly in its direction—man and thrall alike. More forest spirits appear from the bushes with murder in their eyes—creatures of every shape and size, made of flesh and blood, rock and wood.

"What is this?" Alanssia demands.

"These damn spirits," Raenia barks. "They stand against us?!"

Clesturia backs away and glances at Nialla and Sackery. "They make their choice."

"No. It's not a choice," Nialla utters, getting to her feet. "They don't have to fear you anymore!"

"Is that so?" Clesturia questions.

"They will die like the dogs they are!" Raenia spouts.

"Are you so sure?" Sackery asks.

More beasts fill the tree line, stepping onto the field . . . hundreds . . . thousands. Far more than the Crows have thralls to spare. Sackery can hear squealing in the woods, an unseen fight as the enemy's army turns against itself, puppets and spirits killing each other. Choosing a side, as Clesturia so kindly stated.

Wolves swarm the clearing's outer circle, killing off any thrall in their way. Human fighters surge forward with spears and lances, attempting to push the Crows' forces from their lines. The Mórhathan lunges forward and wraps its jaw around a thrall's chest, splitting the unfortunate thing into halves. Several others are caught in the fury, dying alongside their allies.

Sackery retreats to Nialla and lends her his arm. Rasterforn and a contingent of his soldiers fight their way to them, believing it's a safer place than remaining close to the war between the Forest and the Crows. They defend against another wave before Rasterforn and Sackery find a moment of respite.

"Glad you're still alive, Vedrethal!" Rasterforn says, clasping him on the shoulder.

Sackery winces. "Don't know for how much longer."

"We should take this chance and fall back!"

"Not until they're dead!" he refuses, pointing at the Crows fighting off countless vengeful spirits.

"And how do you propose we do that? I've lost half my men!" Rasterforn argues.

Sackery opens his mouth but stops when he feels the thuds of the monster's heavy footfalls. The Mórhathan approaches, spitting out a meaty chuck it took from its massacre. Red lumps dot its bark-like skin, like scars. A hundred battles it's fought and won, the wounds healing over time. Sackery takes in his reflection through the creature's dull amber eyes. The beast takes a step forward. Then another. It growls and snarls, causing the Maheirans beside Sackery to inch backward. Urine runs down their trousers, dousing their boots.

The Mórhathan's glare mellows as its posture shifts unthreateningly to gawk at Nialla behind them. Sackery shifts to see the girl smiling at the creature, her pupils bright and full, unbroken like the sun on a clear day. And in a terrifying moment, the bear draws back and sits on its hind legs.

"What's happening?" a soldier begs the question.

"Offering a choice of my own," Nialla answers.

"To whom?"

"All of them."

She pushes through the crowd, humming a soft little lullaby.

Sackery recognizes the song. It's what the girl's mother sang to her at night as a baby. The sound gradually builds across the field surrounding Assildrusk. All the fighting stops. Human soldiers, their enemy thralls, and even the forest spirits . . . They all listen.

Cyridel finds Sackery in the chaos and clenches his arm.

One by one, the thralls drop to the ground, their strings cut by Nialla's voice. *Free.* Sand spills from their mouths.

Sackery notices Clesturia, Alanssia, and Raenia through the mist, their eyes red.

Raenia darts forward in a blur, catching the Vedrethal by

the throat and dragging him toward her sisters. Rasterforn charges with his soldiers, but Alanssia moves to protect the former, collapsing the chest plates of several and crushing their ribs, killing them.

"Stay back!" Alanssia shouts.

Rasterforn stops with the remainder of his men. "Why?"

"Because I will kill him," Raenia threatens, tightening her grip on Sackery, causing him to gasp for air.

Sackery kicks at her knee, surprising her. He rolls away and takes a spear off the ground, thrusting it where her jaw meets her neck.

Raenia belches as blood spews from her mouth. Sackery draws the spear back, throwing it again, piercing her torso at the heart. Her body hits the cold, hard dirt, her eyes pale.

Alanssia looks on with horror. "Murderer!"

The Mórhathan attacks the woman before she can respond, trampling her into the mud. Alanssia screeches, pounding on the creature's thick hide, but even *she* can't hurt the damn thing.

Clesturia sprints to intercede. Gallandhal, watching from above, dives toward her and shreds the woman's face with beak and talons.

Alanssia forces the bear to drop her, scratching at its eyes, only for Assildrusk to bravely act upon the chance.

The tree stretches with all its many limbs and ensnares Alanssia. Before the woman could fight it off, the weodemair impales her through the abdomen with its roots. The tree groans loudly and cheers as it lifts and tosses the corpse into the woods. An incredible array of sounds follows—snorts and grunts, smacking, and teeth grinding. A veritable feast for all the creatures the witches tormented in their centuries of dominion over the Seclumor Wilds.

Sackery pulls the spear from Raenia, lifting his head to watch.

Clesturia is now completely alone. She catches Gallandhal by the wings and tosses the white bird aside.

Bloodied and hurt, the final sister clearly shows her fear. The witch hadn't guessed how the forest would stand defiantly with Nialla, for she is Vedreron. She is a child to the singers of the songs that shaped every world and star across the great black sky.

"Defeated by a mewling runt? How?!" Clesturia asks, dropping to her knees, lips trembling.

Sackery lets out his breath, seeing the tears in the woman's eyes. It's a hard thing to witness, even for him.

Nialla walks to her, slow but steady. "My mother once said that we are the sums of our bonds," she tells her. "Even when our chains break, the links that connect us somehow endure. It doesn't matter their distance from one another. They're still a part of the same strand holding two ends together."

"There's nothing left holding me," Clesturia weeps. "Only my hate." Her eyes fall sharply from Nialla.

"Your hate? Your pain," Nialla counts. "All of it a struggle?"

"We dared fate, little one," Clesturia describes. "We had no control. They abandoned us."

"You were victims," Sackery offers a kind word.

Clesturia laughs. "Says the man raised as a killer since boyhood."

"I did my duty," Sackery grimaces.

"A lie you repeat until it's all you know how to say."

"Would I be here if I didn't believe it?"

"Would any of us be?"

Sackery angrily steps toward her, only for Rasterforn to block his way. His soldiers encircle the witch, their weapons glistening in the faint light that breaks through the wild canopy above Mireaderal. The Mórhathan lumbers between Clesturia and Nialla, growling in a threatening tone, clearly wanting to protect the girl.

"Our past doesn't matter anymore," Nialla tells her.

"You can't forget decades of torture by a man you trusted," Clesturia mourns.

"Why not? All it takes is the courage to move on."

"Life is not a fairy tale, little one."

"You are who you choose to be," Nialla denies. "But can you be forgiven?"

"Do you think I deserve it?" Clesturia taunts.

"No. I am not the only one you've hurt," Nialla frowns. "You did terrible things to so many."

"Meaning you'll leave my life in the hands of those who hate me," the other laughs.

Nialla warmly smiles. "Do you know I've never had anywhere to call home all these years? Nowhere to feel safe after dark, that is . . . I like to dream about dancing in yellow fields when the sun reaches midday," she faithfully describes. Clesturia's eyes widen, listening with intent. "I dream about swimming in a lake someday, floating there, aimlessly, unbothered by those who'd see me as easy prey."

Her words reverberate throughout the field under the weodemair, strengthening the nearby greenery. Withered trees grow new buds, and flowers sing as they do before their blooms take hold, responding to the girl's soft voice.

Sackery drops back. Rasterforn catches him and eases him to the ground.

Nialla looks at him and nods.

"Foolish dreams? But I only have nightmares," Clesturia smolders, lifting her head. "Because I am afraid? Here, at the end, I . . . I don't have the strength. Yet if you let me go, you may find that life, little one. Make it real. You won't see me again. I promise."

Nialla looks to the Mórhathan. "You can't promise anything."

"Are you a killer, then?" Clesturia demands. "Alike your guardian?

"Maybe I am if I allow myself to be," Nialla suggests. "But your life isn't mine."

"You'll learn . . . Someday, you will face it," Clesturia seethes. "All that rage? That feeling of powerlessness? You will call on it—"

"Enough!" Sackery attempts to intercede.

"—And when you do, it will feel so good. You'll lose yourself, Nialla. As I did."

"He said enough!" Rasterforn shouts, marching forward and plunging his sword into her chest.

Clesturia's voice dies. Her influence quickly fades as she slumps over to her side, her eyes dull against the black.

"I will always wonder who I am, no doubt about that. None," Nialla tells the empty husk.

Cyridel runs and wraps her arms around the girl as the mist clears the air. The Maheirans look at them in wonderment, unsure what to do. Sackery pushes off the ground with Rasterforn's assistance, who leads him to a clear patch without so many bodies. The Mórhathan clamps its jaws around Clesturia's neck, dragging her remains as it leads the other spirits away from the battle's survivors.

The bear looks back at Nialla one last time before disappearing into the Wilds.

Sackery breathes as the pain in his side hits him. "Are we done?" he asks.

"Looks like you cracked a few ribs," Rasterforn tells him. "But by this good earth, we made it."

Sackery removes his armor, unbuckling the belts that hold the pieces together, and sets them aside. Rasterforn helps.

"Not all of us," Sackery coughs. "Life has a funny way of making us pay for our mistakes."

"Seems we all paid for it in the end," Rasterforn frowns.

Sackery winces as he lowers his arms. It's not the worst he's felt after a fight, but it's also not his best. Corpses lay atop corpses across the meadow.

Rasterforn's people took a heavy toll to rescue him. How many died? Sackery doesn't even know their names.

"I am sorry," he tells the man.

"What for? We didn't do this for you."

"But your people died?"

"They died fighting for a home to call theirs."

The man smirks and shakes his head. Rasterforn finishes wrapping Sackery's wounds and takes a seat next to him.

"I couldn't keep my promise," Sackery sighs.

"And it would be unfair for me to hold that against you," Rasterforn admits. "Do you see that?" The man points at Nialla in the crowd, helping her mother comb through the survivors. "That girl of yours? She was adamant in marching out here and taking on those damn Crows. All to save your desperate ass."

"She's stubborn that way—"

"Like her father?"

"I am not her father," Sackery chuckles. "Oh, that hurts."

"No. I mean Endúcar," Rasterforn corrects.

Sackery purses his lips. "She told you," he realizes.

"A white bird sang a little tune," Rasterforn tells him. "Gallandhal? All the pieces fell into place."

Sackery looks upward and finds the Shanashéron in the treetops. The bird seems brighter after the fight with Clesturia. At least brighter than when he met her in the woods. With the air clear, Sackery expects life to return to this valley and the weodemair tree that feeds it.

"She warned me," Sackery explains, "and I didn't listen."

"And what will you do now?" Rasterforn asks.

"Help clean up this mess," he offers.

"You can barely stand."

"I'll be all right."

"And you call the girl stubborn."

Sackery scoffs as he rises to his feet.

He falls backward into the mud, and his world darkens. Sackery only catches glimpses of what happens next . . . Two riders approach and lift him into a saddle. They tie straps around him in case he loses consciousness. Nialla stays with him before getting lifted onto a second horse with another rider. All the while, the girl holds his hand.

She tugs on his shirt as the riders jeer their mounts full sprint on the return to the city.

Sackery doesn't recall the days between Mireaderal and Trebunor. It's all a haze. He wants a thick wool blanket over him and a feather pillow under his head whenever he awakes. And he wouldn't turn down a hot bowl of soup with boiled chicken . . . Maybe a slice or two of apple pie? Trebunor had plentiful apple trees and orchards before its collapse. Perhaps the fruit will grow again?

"Don't worry, old man," a voice breaks through. "We're almost there. Home."

Home. That's the word for it.

Everything they fought for, where this journey of theirs ends.

A LIFE OF LOVE

Nialla sits at his bedside on a newly made chair. She wraps her arms around her legs with her chin on her knees.

Rasterforn's people have set up this room for the wounded—laying furs across the stone floor, dragging braziers in from the city. They've kept the embers warm, making the air comfortable for Sackery and the others.

Sackery has lain on the bed, under wool blankets, for nine days now, regaining his strength.

He asks for soup and pie almost daily, but the best the cooks can do is give him chicken broth with floating chunks.

Rasterforn had his riders carry him to Trebunor. The commander caught up with them a few mornings after with the other survivors. Nialla heard that some folk were still missing from the battle's aftermath, either dead or had wandered off into the woods. The search is ongoing for them, but there isn't much hope.

Her mother helps the injured as the days go by. She threads needles, applies bandages, and treats the more severe cases with *virrenroot*, which grows abundantly in the city's gardens.

"When did you learn to do that?" Nialla asks her at one point.

Cyridel happily grins. "After I met your father, he needed constant attention," she explains, folding clean linens. "Imagine doing this for months? Thankfully, I wasn't his only caretaker. One of the Madi Ilivari—Ilhivendal's healer chore—watched him when I had to sleep."

"You weren't a healer before?" Nialla asks.

"No. I was a light-footed child who liked to dance in the river," her mother confides. "But my father challenged me to the task. He never explained why, even after I asked him. Then, he left Ilhivendal to find answers to more pressing questions. For three months, I was diligent in my chores. I did my duty as my father's daughter."

"Until my father awoke."

Her mother pauses for a moment and frowns. Her eyes lose their warmth like she's remembering unhappy thoughts.

"Until he awoke," she whispers, fighting every tear. "And the man Taherian Endúcar became Galron of the Hiírom, the First of Men."

Nialla recalls the stories her mother told of whenever her father spoke, a room would fall quiet and listen.

Sackery stirs under his covers as her mother walks away.

Nialla sits up and looks at him, wide-eyed and nosy. *Can he talk?* They've not had many opportunities to discuss what happened at Mireaderal. He's slept for days, never awake for more than a few hours before dozing off again. It's hard to look at him like this, a broken old warrior with his prime years behind him.

This time . . . his eyes flutter open. Sackery looks . . . confused. His gaze wanders like a newborn fox until it eventually lands on Nialla beside him.

"Why are you still here?" he asks, quiet as a shallow grave.

"I never left," Nialla tells him.

Sackery smiles. "You should be out in the sun. It looks like a beautiful day."

"There's enough light in here," she smirks.

"Embers. Not a light you can grow old in," he laments.

"It's not so bad," Nialla admits.

Sackery looks at her with sorrow in his eyes. "Why did you follow me? It was dangerous."

"Because if I didn't, I would have lost you. What you did wasn't brave. It was stupid. Reckless."

He lets off a chuckle. "Much like going after *me* was reckless," Sackery issues. "But then . . . I suppose you *did* learn from me . . . I am . . . What's the phrase? A stupid, stupid man?" Talking causes his ribs to convulse, making him cough. Nialla flinches when he does. He clenches his side before sitting up against the backboard. "Your mother was right. Maybe I am getting too old to play the wanderer?"

"How old are you anyway?" Nialla jests. "More than a tree, less than a mountain—?"

"I don't need any more reminders, thank you very much." Sackery holds out his hands and surrenders. He lies back down with a weakness in his chest. His muscles have yet to recover, but he will stand and walk again sooner than later. "Still strong enough to win the fight."

"They had you chained to a rock!" Nialla laughs.

"But you didn't see what they had to throw at me to do it."

"They wore you down, did they?"

"Like three strumpets in Umbridge. Big ladies."

"Gross."

"I merely tell how it is, Nells."

He has his humor back.

"And how do you feel now?" she asks.

"Like I wrestled a bear and went back for seconds," Sackery coughs. "What's happened?"

"King Rasterforn's working to secure his position in the city," Nialla tells him.

"Rasterforn? A king now?" Sackery begs the question.

"His people declared it three days ago," Nialla explains. "I think they intend to stay."

"An easy choice with the threat now gone," Sackery reassures. "Trebunor has good earth, a defensible position, and ready access to the rivers. The Maithandír had chosen it for a reason. If his people can make it work, the city will be a good foundation for expanding their borders throughout the valley. Turn it into something that makes them proud."

"And by the sounds of it, a few want to join us when we leave," Nialla breaks the news.

Sackery draws his head to one side as she mentions it, less than happy. "Coming with us?" When we—?" He lies there, taking in a heavy breath. Nialla can see the concern on his face as he searches for the right words.

"I cannot hide what I am from them," Nialla confides. "Not after everything we did. They aim to join us at Wilhimusk."

"You told them about it?"

"And why not? You said we could start a new life there. Build ourselves—"

"A home? Yes. Home," Sackery finishes, bouncing the word on his tongue. "Wilhimusk. It'll be risky for us, Nells, taking them with."

Nialla rises out of her chair in protest. "And if it weren't for them, we'd never have beaten the Crows. So many died. A lot still don't know why." She stands her ground, putting a foot down and making the decision. "But I know we can trust them. Those coming with us, at least."

"Rasterforn didn't march to Mireaderal for me," Sackery tells her. "A threat was at his door. He needed it dead."

"No. He went for me!" Nialla denies. "It was the right thing to do!"

"Because he knows *what* you are, *what* you can do for him," Sackery argues.

"Is that a bad thing? Don't you think it's worth giving them the benefit of the doubt?"

"Maybe?" he only half agrees, releasing a sigh. "But how much more will we have to sacrifice for them?"

"As much as they'll sacrifice for us," Nialla says, drawing the line.

Sackery laughs at her temper. He coughs painfully afterward. Nialla drops back into her chair, feeling guilty.

"I suppose I don't have a choice in this, do I?" he asks, surrendering the argument.

"No. We already said we'd be glad for the company," Nialla admits, firm and triumphant.

"And your mother?"

"Preparing for the journey. Once you're able to stand?"

"We'll head out," Sackery agrees. "Put our feet on the road to Wilhimusk."

— 22 —

DANCING IN THE LIGHT

Cyridel tightens the buckle, securing her gear behind the saddle. They won't leave for another day or two, but it's never too early to prepare some minor provisions. Mrillane and Desre have gifted Cyridel a few choice items she's gone without in the decades since she departed from Ilhivendal.

Yeavengeritt hands her the satchel. She opens it, sneaking a whiff of a waxy soap bar, savoring the redolence.

"It smells like nectar and torrid pines," Cyridel tells Yeavengeritt.

"The ladies tell me they picked it up in Hanna," he explains.

"It sounds nice, wherever that is."

Cyridel smiles at him before tying off the top of the sack.

Her mare burrs as Cyridel pats the creature's snout. It's a mild beast—not an animal that should ever get thrown into war, yet that's where she comes from. Her master died in the fighting at Mireaderal. A spear threw him off while this one ran into the underbrush. Cut and bruised. Nothing that won't heal in time.

"Ais'emón manüra, leú veshiallé," she whispers to comfort her. "Kál earna yülin iné il hüns vantian aoanin."

The creature happily stirs when Cyridel speaks.

It's all right, my friend, it meant. *The road ahead will be ours together now.*

Cyridel finds it strange how animals can understand her native Aarendelic despite being raised under a more common tongue.

"Her name is Ora," Rasterforn says, walking into the barn. "She's a mellow beast and listens well. Treat her like family, Daughter of Ilhivendal."

Yeavengeritt looks at the man, bows, and quietly bids Cyridel his leave.

"She's mournful," Cyridel frowns.

"Her former master brought her up since she was a foal," Rasterforn explains. "Not a warhorse. Her sire was a beast of burden, tilling wheat fields. Quite the journey she's been on, full of adventure. Not the kind meant for the timid-hearted."

"Somebody should write a book about it," Cyridel suggests.

"Ora the Yellow, maybe? Decent title," Rasterforn offers. "A tale for children."

"I'd like 'A Walk Across Yellow Fields,' instead," Cyridel counters. "We're a far cry from any farm she'd know."

"That we are," the man agrees.

Rasterforn walks up and runs a hand through the mare's long mane, smiling at Cyridel. Eventually, his eyes meet hers.

"Everything's almost ready to go," Cyridel says, stepping away.

"Are you sure about leaving?" Rasterforn asks.

"Sackery's on his feet, his wounds mostly healed," she lists.

"That doesn't answer the question, Lady Miralifrim," the man frowns.

Cyridel forces a smile as she admits, "Yes."

"You four can stay with us for as long as you'd like," Raster-forn offers. "It'll be no trouble. You'll be safe."

"I wish it were so easy. We've been on our own for over sixty years," Cyridel remarks. "Nowhere is safe. My daughter draws many dangers to her. We avoided them because we kept on the move, never staying anywhere for longer than a few days. But to settle down? I suspect a few will finally catch up to us, whatever their intent. And we must be ready when they do."

Rasterforn's eyes fall groundward. Whether the man doesn't understand her or because he's afraid of what's ahead, she can't guess.

He eventually nods, rubbing his palms together. "And how *is* Master Greywolfe?"

"Sackery? I have known the man for decades," Cyridel tells him. King Rasterforn, his people call him now. But he is a monarch without a kingdom or much of a country, even after the hard-won battle with the Crows. Rasterforn's hold over the valley is delicate. "It's difficult to see him like that. Hurt. Not wholly broken, but not intact, either."

"Not broken," Rasterforn winks. "Greywolfe is a soldier. A good man."

Cyridel looks at him with surprise. "A soldier? You think he's still just a soldier?"

"That's what the Vedrethal are, aren't they? Soldiers for a war that ended years ago. Now they wander the countryside, helping some, aggravating many others, killing monsters. Enacting their justice, whatever that means. Protecting villages and little girls from the great evils in the world."

"Some would call them heroes," Cyridel describes him.

"And does he view himself as a hero?" Rasterforn begs the question.

Cyridel rolls a blanket and tucks it behind her mare's saddle seat. "Does it matter what he calls himself?"

"Killer is the word he told me," Rasterforn confesses. "Warrior-servants? Scholars, fighters to the last . . . Men and women? Defenders of a cause that nobody remembers. The Crows? They understood better than most what titles cost for those like him."

Rasterforn and Sackery are soldiers with blood on their hands. Cyridel does not doubt that. *But what is the difference between a soldier and a leader?* A soldier kills when he needs to. A leader convinces others that it is necessary.

Cyridel looks into the man's eyes and reads the scars, not in the flesh, but in his soul. Every battle he's fought has a tale, with faces he wants to forget.

"Is that your attempt to convince me to stay?" she asks.

"I—? No, that's not what I meant," Rasterforn sighs.

"Then speak your mind," Cyridel urges him.

The man squares his shoulders and clears his throat. "I want you to stay with us," he speaks.

"Raster—?"

"But such are our fates, Cyridel Elendsah," Rasterforn admits. "To ask you again would break my heart when I already know the answer. Much as I know your people can only love once, your love already belongs to a man far greater than me." He sucks in his gut and takes a wavered breath.

Cyridel's face brightens as she rests a hand on the man's shoulder.

"Often what we want is never what we need," she offers him, only for the king to pull away.

"I do have something for you to give the Vedrethal after you set out," Rasterforn says. He walks to the barn's entry and reaches behind the doors, only to pull out a sword wrapped in cloth. Sackery had lost Myheirad when the Crows wore him down. "A small reminder of a home far away."

Cyridel accepts the gift and unwraps it, drawing the blade.

"This steel? Míran-forged," she recognizes it. "See how it's folded? Where did you get this?"

"From Nrondon," Rasterforn affirms. "It's not Ilhivendal, but—?"

"We can't accept this," Cyridel shakes her head, reseating

the blade in its sheath.

Rasterforn eyes her with an amused demeanor before his lips crack. "A warrior without a weapon is like a river without water," the man claims. "Empty. And if what you say is true, that your daughter is in danger, then her greatest protector needs a tool to defend her with." He closes her hands around the sword in the cloth.

Cyridel feels the edges crease her palms. "Do you know its name?" she decides to ask.

The man flips a corner of the cloth and points at an inscription etched into the crossguard. "Something I am not familiar with," Rasterforn says with a modest chuckle. "But I do believe *you* can read it. Aarendelic? A form of elvish outside my tutelage."

She runs her thumb across the letterforms. "That's because the metal's worn," Cyridel tells him, turning the blade so he can see it.

"Then it's an old sword?"

"Or it's passed through many hands."

"Can you make out what it says?"

Cyridel turns back the blade and squints. "Aru il Endril," she thinks it reads.

"And what does that mean?"

"Could be the name of its original master."

"Sackery wouldn't mind wielding another's sword?"

"Taking up a fellow soldier's weapon is an honorable act for my kind," Cyridel describes. She pulls away and finds a snug place for it in her saddle. "It's like accepting a life debt to your brother-in-arms, a promise to stand where they fell, holding the line against the enemy." Cyridel will present it to Sackery on the road when he feels strong enough to wield it.

Rasterforn kindly smiles. "I did not know that about your people."

"That's what my brother, Erathil, told me," Cyridel confesses.

"And will Master Greywolfe consider it an honor?"

"Yes. And I cannot thank you enough, King Rasterforn. Not many are so generous."

That sets a glow on the man's face. It is as if she has given him the confidence to welcome the title, as much as he no doubt feels the burden it has on men like him. Rasterforn and his people journeyed to Trebunor to escape the politics that destroyed their previous lives. For him to ascend to kingship with only a few thousand settlers in a ruined city?

"I am not much of a king of anything yet," Rasterforn admits.

"A ruler leads his people, not the land they sit on," Cyridel suggests.

"His people? Then let me declare the Men of Sordon will always have a place for you."

"Sordon?"

"It's what my people will call this valley," Rasterforn explains. "We are now the Sordheiran by popular decree."

"Then by your leave, King of the Sordheiran, Lord of Trebunor," Cyridel mocks him.

"Don't jest with me, Lady Miralifrim," the man veers.

Cyridel laughs. "And who *can* I jest with? Sackery? My daughter?"

"Neither come off as particularly cheerful," he winces.

Cyridel raises her hands and offers him a curtsy. "As you please."

"Safe travels to wherever you find home, my lady," Rasterforn returns a bow.

He then departs without saying another word. His eyes glow as he steps through the doors, looking back for only a beat before disappearing entirely. That is the pride he's feeling right now. Purpose? It rolls off him like a warm summer scent.

She returns to grooming Ora, her mare. Whatever tomorrow brings, it is the beginning of a new day. They will set out for Wilhimusk and build their Houdicar, their home atop the Greencliffs, high enough to see the world.

Cyridel notices the brilliant amaryllis petals blooming red around the dead weodemair tree as she walks outside. With the Crows defeated, life returns to Trebunor and the Seclumor Wilds—birds singing in the air, children running gleefully in the streets. And no trace of the cold that penetrated every nook of this broken city.

Hope comes from the most unexpected things. Sometimes, all they need to do is walk across a bridge.

– Rasterforn and Cyridel –

— 23 —

THE HEIGHTS ABOVE WILHIMUSK

Sackery rides ahead when the cliffs rise alongside the mountains. He's never been so glad to see them again. The snowcapped peaks reflect the sunlight there, glowing like beacons across the valley's mouth for many leagues.

Nothing's changed.

The last time he walked this country was on his hunt for Icurian. Sackery tracked his father for decades. It was here where the two finally caught up with each other. Something drew the Doomed King to this place. It wasn't until now that Sackery understood his reasons for coming this far south.

He presses his palm into his chest. "Never thought I'd return. My home away from home, as you'd say."

"Home is where you feel safest," Cyridel remarks, stopping beside him. "You were fighting to end a war, Sackery, my friend."

Sackery looks at her with a pain in his throat. "Not that it mattered," he tells her. "No matter how hard I fought, my path led me to a circle. I am where I thought it ended." He clicks his tongue and slows his horse.

He counts the upturned rocks along the approach to the Greencliffs and moves past the fissures dotting the landscape, left as wounds. Sackery stood here when Icurian lashed out at him, a fight that lasted days, with neither father nor son knowing when to yield. Even in defeat, the Doomed King was a powerful force.

Sackery looks at the caravan following his road. Hundreds came with him from Trebunor, climbing over the hills.

He doesn't know how he feels about that . . . *Is it good?* Or is he scared, like that boy on the ship crossing from Islinin?

A little river flows from farther up the valley. The current is slow and pleasant, wildflowers brimming the embankments. There's a strong smell of lavender carried by the wind, abundant fruit trees, and bushes of purple mulberries growing along the hills and cliffsides.

Sackery wanted to retire here when the war between Heluvian and Icurian had ended. Fate wasn't on his side. He committed to the Watchful Rest with the remainder of the Vedrethal inside the Grandir Halls under the Aronur Mountains. Every moment was an eternity, unable to move, breathe, or blink. His lungs screamed desperately for fresh air—a thousand years to allow the world to pass them by and forget.

How does a man not lose his purpose after living with that curse? Sackery wonders silently.

He looks at Nialla riding with the other children, keeping them entertained on the journey.

She is the one who gives him a reason to keep walking on a path he has already trodden. And when she turns to him, he smiles, like a father to a daughter that's not *his* to love. But he does love her, his Lady of the Mountains. The one good thing that came out of Icurian's plans to "save the world," as the man so audaciously claimed.

Reaching the first bend to the steps of the Greencliffs, Sackery dismounts his horse. Nialla and Cyridel do the same, taking his hand as they walk the winding path. The others wave at them as they climb, the first cheers filling the air of their new home.

Nialla waves back at them, letting out a whistle that sounds over the fields below.

He squeezes her arm and calls out, his voice rising with hers in a serenade that will forever mark this moment in their songs.

At the very top, there's a small lake etched into the flat plateau, surrounded by long grass and bright flowers. Fear of the dark vanishes up here so close to the sun and far below the mountain snows. The settlers who've journeyed with them begin erecting a camp on the hill at the base of the cliffs—Wilhimusk, as they'll know it.

And this high above the fields, the people appear like ants, small and busy.

Cyridel puts a hand on his shoulder. "This will do."

Nialla looks over the pond, running her fingers through the still waters.

Sackery stares at her. "We are isolated here," he confides.

"It's very pretty," the girl agrees.

"We have a good view of the surrounding hills," Cyridel identifies, tracing the horizon with her thumb.

"And will notice anyone approaching us for miles," Sackery agrees.

He can make this place safe for them without fearing the hunters on their trail.

Nialla runs toward them and stomps her foot on a clear patch of earth. "Can we build our house up here?"

"A small house," Sackery laughs. "Materials will need carrying up the trail. It's a steep climb. Tents will do us for now."

The girl smiles, accepting the proposal. Cyridel kneels to her, and together, they hold up their hands, counting the spaces between the hills and bends.

As above, so below. Sackery notions.

He is Sackery Greywolfe, defender of Nialla Elendsah, the Lady of the Mountains.

And she is the only reason he is still alive.

— 24 —

A SIGHT, UNEXPECTED

Verhan sifts the sand in his gloved palm, mixed with black dirt—blood, left over by the fight.

Some of the bodies remain, those few the survivors in Trebunor decided not to collect. Enemies? Or were they merely forgotten in the long haul to return the fallen to their families? He doesn't know. But he shouldn't guess at the misfortune of those left behind.

He sprinkles the last of the soil and smells the leather of his glove after. It has a sourness to it, weeks old. But there's . . . something else. A bright tinge on the air, constant and familiar. "Seems others did our task for us."

The ground rumbles as his . . . well, it would be too much to call the man a friend. Comrade? In whatever case, the *other* walks to the weodemair tree in the middle of the field and lays his forehead against its trunk. The old tree vibrates and burrs, raising its branches high into the air as if answering the sun's warmth.

"Such be our luck to fall a step behind," Icurian announces.

Verhan stands up and circles the dais, following the tracks of armored boots imprinted on the ground. "Is that what you call this?"

The other turns away from him with a guilt heavy on his shoulders. "Yes," Icurian mourns.

"No less lost for words, I see," Verhan tells the man. "Then what do you make of these?" He stops at the skeletal remains left behind by the battle, the flesh melting into the ground. Hack marks on the bones show where the blades hit and killed the creature, a merciful end to a thrall that shouldn't have been able to walk.

The other comes alongside him and kneels. "Puppets. Filled with sand," Icurian describes.

"And how many did they control?"

"Hundreds? Thousands? It's quite effortless."

"You know that from experience?"

"No. Even at my lowest, there were things I considered myself above."

He looks side-eyed at the man and frowns, unwilling to believe him—Icurian, the Exiled. "Had we only arrived sooner?"

"Perhaps our delay was by luck? Even without us, the world looks for balance."

"These people did not have to fight alone."

"But *were* they alone?"

Verhan scoffs and stands, looking for the tracks in the dirt to allow him to follow the battle's course.

It was a chaotic fight, with an ebb to the lines that suggested an intense back and forth. One side would take advantage over the other, only for the tide to shift as reinforcements came from the deep wilds. And with trace signs of a beast, like a bear, but larger than any bear he knows from his travels.

Did the duo come here for no reason?

Verhan found the other decades ago, aggrieved, broken by his exile. Hardly anything of the Doomed King left inside him, a shade of the man once his enemy.

The world is an unkind place for even the mightiest of the mighty.

And these witches, the Crows, had to learn that for themselves. Icurian wanted to talk to them, to set things right. Undo his mistake with them, or finally put them out of their misery. Icurian never said *what* that mistake was. All he spoke about was their betrayal of him near the end of his terror. He sought revenge then, even when he could least afford it.

Looking at the other, Verhan squeezes his wrist, feeling the skin under his glove sting. "No. I sense it, too. Whispers in the rocks?"

Icurian nods. "Someone like us, there is no mistake."

The other presses his hand into the dirt and squeezes, offering a small hum before drawing his arm back and letting out his breath. All the soil, the leaves, and the rocks shake and shift, gathering in clumps that re-formed as dusty figures, mirroring real people from the battle.

"What is this?" Verhan asks.

"Echoes of the past," Icurian answers.

"How?"

"Assildrusk remembers."

Icurian whistles. The earth blooms like a dance, and the dancers wield spears and shields. All the figures crash into an onslaught. Verhan follows the flow of it, the soldiers filling the field, the horse riders charging at the earliest onset to push toward the center, toward . . . A man chained to a boulder on the far side.

Verhan stops and watches as a little girl runs to him, frees the chained man, and collapses in his arms.

It all lasted mere seconds, but the sense remains a strong one. Verhan loses his breath, knowing *that* face, *her* face. No. He can't look at this.

He steers away and marches into the woods. Icurian chases after him, catching his shoulder, only for Verhan to pull away. "Master Endúcar!" the other demands. "What is the matter with you?" Icurian takes him by his shirt and pins him against a tree. "Breathe. What did you see?"

Verhan swallows and pushes the other off him. "I don't—" He stops as he spies a long, sharp metal rod sticking out of the dirt.

Icurian traces his gaze and goes to pick it up, brushing it off with his sleeve. "Myheirad?" he says in utter shock.

"It's a hard thing to mistake," Verhan agrees.

Icurian flips the blade to its side and hands him the hilt. "The last time I saw this sword?"

"It was during our battle in the Grandir Halls," Verhan describes. "Sackery of the Vedrethal?" He takes the sword and tilts the edge to see the reflection of his silver eyes in the steel. "His blade. The man who fought with me during the Battle of Aardan against the dragon Morenarch."

"That means your daughter is also here," Icurian cautions.

"That little girl in the echo—"

"They are the ones who beat the Crows."

"Which means we are putting them in danger the longer we stay here."

"On that, Endúcar, we agree," Icurian nods.

Verhan hands the sword back to the other before returning to the field. "Isn't there more we can do?"

"Not without drawing their attention," Icurian denies. "And I know you, Endúcar."

"It is better they believe I am dead."

"Better for who?"

"For my daughter? For Cyridel?"

"She will come looking for you someday."

"But not before she's lived a happy life away from us."

Icurian's face darkens like he does not believe him. "Look around at this meadow, Endúcar. Do you think your daughter is safe when my mistakes haunt us? And what happens if our enemies discover her? She can't hide what she is forever. Others will hear her songs, much as we do now."

"She's too young to understand."

"Or you're too afraid to confront a mistake as I do."

Verhan surrenders a scornful glare before waving him off, unapologetic to a man who destroyed so much. But he can't ignore the wisdom in Icurian's words. As wrong as the man's been for so much of his life, he isn't wrong now, as much that puts a foul taste in his mouth to admit.

"I *am* afraid," he admits.

Vanhashal lands on a tree branch above them, taking the form of a white eagle—a Shanashéron, bright and pristine as glass in starlight. Verhan smiles at the bird until a second one finds a perch next to him, the trim of its feathers disheveled, with its glow cracked and faded.

Icurian raises his head and draws back a step. "Another one?"

"Shanashé don't usually fly together," Verhan offers the thought. "Odd to find two following us. And this one? She seems—"

"Wounded? Yes. Her name is Gallandhal," Icurian tells him.

"You know her?"

"She is a friend from years ago. Much like Vanhashal is to you, Master Endúcar."

"What happened to her?"

"I left her behind when I abandoned Clesturia, Alanssia,

and Raenia to their fate. Another mistake."

"None of us can change the past."

Icurian lowers his head to the two shanashéron and leaves for the old forest road soon after. "Not all of us must resign to what strings hold us," he says. Verhan doesn't follow him. Not at first. He looks up at the white birds, their violet, almost purple eyes peering down at him like four tiny stars judging him. "Leave them, Endúcar! Until next time."

Vanhashal offers him an encouraging nod before turning to Gallandhal.

The faded bird doesn't break away, almost as if she wants to speak out but is reluctant.

"I will return when the moment is right," Verhan tells her.

"Then I will watch over her until you do," Gallandhal promises.

Verhan smiles and offers her a bow. It's all he can do to keep Nialla safe from the greatest dangers that hunt their kind. Clesturia, Alanssia, and Raenia were only discarded remnants of a war that nobody remembers anymore. Their unity was their strength, but they were weak, the lowest Vedr who once served Icurian.

Another war will come, with players with a head for longer games.

Nialla, his daughter, is the one thing he hopes to spare from the battles ahead.

Icurian claims she can't escape it. Nialla will see enough death in her life to leave her broken thrice over.

Verhan looks at the field surrounding the weodemair tree, what *she* did to the witches, mad in their power, and what *she* inspired others to do . . . Maybe Icurian's right? And if he is, *that* scares him. All his sacrifices are for nothing if it only makes things worse for her.

He will die before he lets that happen.

Fate brings tragic circumstances that lead the fearful and lost down unknown paths to where they must find themselves.

VEDR, VEDRERON, AND VEDRETHAL

What is a concept? Language manifested into ideas. Pointed fact is my use of uncommon names for places, characters, and objects to illustrate those ideas in a larger narrative. The development of language always fascinated me as a kid. As somebody who grew up without much physical ability to speak, I created new words to complement how my tongue strings syllables together. One of these earliest words was "Vedrethal"–symbolic of a vision I had for a caste of warriors, soldiers, and heroes that could portray the grit of reality as much as the fantastic idealism integral to the fantasy genre.

The kind of protagonist I wanted for my stories was a fighter who could stand a cut above the rest, a sentinel on the wall, or a wanderer who journeys between hamlets, lending a hand or slaying the occasional beast or bandit along the way like in the Arthurian Legends. Maybe a story requires a personal bodyguard for a king or queen? Or a drifter acting as a spy during some political rife between kingdoms? Vedrethal, as a writer, is my word for the classic adventurer archetype, a key player of whatever story I tell within A Tale Beyond Return.

Inspiration, derived from "Vanguard," and used to fill the character role of a wayward order of the knight-errant, the outcast Spartan of Ancient Greece, the Ronin of Japan, or, to contrast, the highly revered Immortals of the Achaemenid Empire, depending on the narrative requirements the particular story I am writing.

As with the old gods and warriors of our real-world mythologies, the Vedrethal share a kindred spirit with the Einherjar (or einheri)—the souls of those who died in battle, carried by the Valkyrie to Valhalla. There, the warriors would train and prepare for Ragnarök, readying themselves for an eventual surge on the fields of Vigrid. In certain stories, the Einherjar served as Odin's chosen to fight by his side at the world's end. A close parallel myth in Ancient Greece is the concept of a warrior fighting for eternal glory. In the former, one would rise to the Great Hall of Asgard by way of the Valkyrie, who would only choose the greatest of slain fighters, while in the Greek myths, the warrior sought to earn the favor of a chosen god, who'd then bring the hero with them to Mount Olympus.

For my work, I wanted a more grounded foundation. Readers can find similarities between the Vedrethal and certain warrior groups throughout European, Japanese, and Middle Eastern historical periods. Knights, for example, were known in chivalric romances for their shining armor and the honor they conducted themselves, even while their real-world counterparts were little better than rich thugs serving in the name of kings or other lords in feudal society. Samurai of Japan are comparable, as a warrior caste that served their daimyo. Like the knights, the Samurai, despite their chivalric code, bushido, which demanded a strict principle to adhere to, often took advantage of their high station by abusing those of lower status. As historical records heavily indicate, commoners viewed these warrior castes with concept.

As I developed the Vedrethal concept, however, I wanted to draw from these historical annals to add a sense of realism to the group—an idealized version of the romances, but capable of that brutal nature. This context is shown in A Tale Beyond Return whenever the Vedrethal are described as "killers" by the opponents they defeat in battle. Now, I prefer the current rendition of the Vedrethal—as warrior-servants, loyal to their duty and sense of justice, but with an underlined horrific past. Vedrethal, trained to fight at a young age, loyal to their master, with a duty-above-self mentality to almost religious levels, and unafraid to make the hard choices, no matter how much disdain they earn from others. Most of all, their sense of unity is intense, treating others of their caste as brothers or sisters, true siblings, due to their many long years of fighting together.

As I cemented these qualities behind my fabled knights and completed more of the comprehensive mythos, close friends raised a question: who do the Vedrethal serve, then? The answer—the Vedrel Lords, as I called them in my earliest notes. Progression of a story's culture is important to avoid the world becoming stale, not only for a fictional narrative but also for real historical context. We see this across records, no matter what culture or people. Names of locations (cities and nations) change according to who occupies the land. As time passed, I would more commonly refer to the Vedrel as the Vedreron after several revisions of the background material, which came to mean "fallen blood" as my shorthand— (originally meant to denote a distinction between the Vedrel and their offspring). Vedreron would feature most prominently with characters Galron and Nialla. Still, I would later use "Vedreron" as a broader descriptive term for their entire race and its members, singular and plural. You are of the Vedreron, so you are Vedreron. And what they are is a matter I debated for some years. They are not gods but rather a complex mixture of entities from the Icelandic sagas and the fallen angels of Christianity, separated by major and minor powers, with factions mirroring the Aesir and Vanir of the Scandinavian peoples (Vedrel and Athen), except with a lot more leeway to define good and evil for individual characterizations.

That would come to define the Vedr, the original members of the Vedreron that fell from Anánturial [Skies Above] at the Second Betrayal by Athulian, the Immaculate. Before they fell to their current sphere, the Vedr stood together as a race called the Aameral, the Singers of the Immortal Songs that Created Life. Akin to when God created the Angels to help him maintain order in the cosmos, Ansolas breathed life into the Aameral to help in the Grand Chorus, crafting new stars and planets from their music. And among them, a few stood taller than most, the Eedian nya Ansolas—Champions of Light.

A key distinction for the reader to recognize the Vedr over other characters is the "ian" or "ia" suffix added to the end of their names—(i.e. Icurian, Nasuria, Heluvian, Alanssia). As the writer, it was important to create this small part of their culture for readers to identify at a glance. In several instances, these characters go by other, more personal names—Aonarfudain for Icurian and Galron for Taherian— which they had chosen for themselves instead of going by how the histories knew them.

Because of their history, the term Old Eedian is sporadically used throughout the text when referring to the Vedr. I would write a character as being from Old Eedian, meaning they were of the Old Champions, who, as previously established, are derived from the Eedian nya Ansolas. Of the Aameral cast out from Anánturial, all were Eedian, the Champions, whom Athulian betrayed. Many were left to wander in unknown lands after the event. They would call themselves Vedr, or "Fallen," with Icurian and Heluvian founding a kingdom then called Old Eedian by the survivors. First, they were a part of Ansolas, the Light. Then, they were the Aameral, Singers of the Immortal Songs. They fought against the Dark Verse brought by Aeterhet as the Eedian nya Ansolas, Champions of Light, at the First Betrayal. Athulian, at the

Second Betrayal, cast them out to a young world where they were the Vedr, the Fallen. Soon after, the Vedreron. After the First War with the Dragons, they raised the initial generation of Vedrethal from the orphaned children of Men and Mírael (or fae), the Aenumorians, a topic for another time.

Names are as important to the storytelling as the very thing they describe. Vedr, Vedreron, and Vedrethal all lend credence to one another. Vedrethal is the first I created in the development, but the last formed within the chronological timeline. From the Vedrethal, new ideas take form, leading to more stories, my version of Arthur's Knights of the Round Table.

– Assildrusk, Lord of the Wilds –

– *Clesturia, The Mother* –